BRADLEY BAKER

and the Gullfather of New York

DAVID LAWRENCE JONES

BRADLEY BAKER

and the Gullfather of New York

The Amazing Adventures of Bradley Baker

BOOK FOUR

Cover illustrated by Abie Greyvenstein

Author's Official Website: bradley-baker.com
Become a fan of Bradley Baker: facebook.com/thebradleybaker

ISBN 978-0-9561499-6-1

2

First published in the UK 2013
Avocado Publishing - Devon United Kingdom
www.avocadopublishing.co.uk

David Lawrence Jones is proud to support

Families for Children
A D O P T I O N

The author would like to recognize all the amazing work carried out
by Families for Children Adoption

Reg. Charity No. 1093131

For more information
http://www.familiesforchildren.org.uk

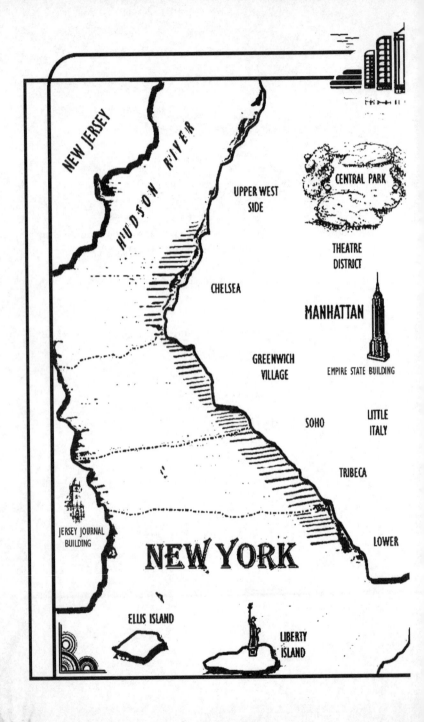

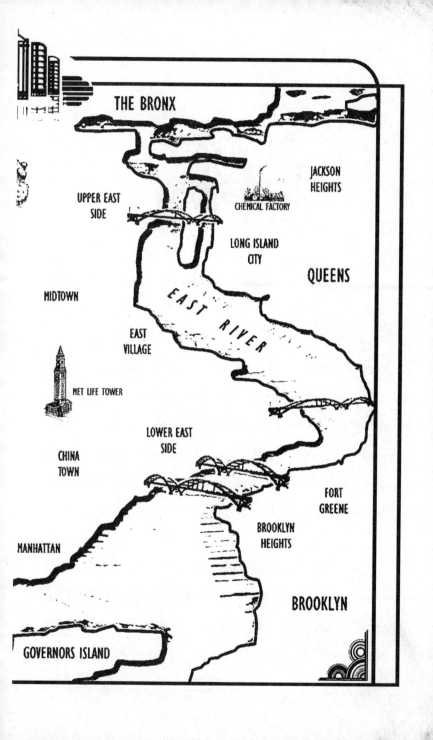

of New York

1

A New Villain

The year was 1916 and a very important date in the world calendar. It was July 30th and Jersey City was about to host the biggest act of espionage in New York's history. Across the Hudson River, the tall buildings of Lower Manhattan stood resplendent, as the moonlight sat low in the clear night sky to portray an iconic cityscape.

This was no ordinary New York skyline; it belonged to a strange city lost in a parallel land far away from the real world and devoid of human inhabitants. It was a dangerous place to live or work;

controlled by familiar bird-like creatures, who governed the streets and policed the roof tops.

However, *a new villain* was about to expose a vulnerable flaw in the city's defenses. Ruthless acts of undercover activities were about to unhinge the judicial hold of governance that secured law and order throughout the great metropolis. The new head of an emerging Mafia syndicate was carefully plotting his reign of terror and planning a series of calculated attacks to gain control of Manhattan.

It was the early hours of a grim smog-filled morning in Jersey City on the west side of the river. The clock on the Jersey Journal Building struck two, as three intimidating figures appeared dressed in trench coats and large trilby hats. The young Mafia boss held out one of his concealed wings and fluttered his feathery hand to summon his two henchmen. The gangsters were working incognito with a group of foreign agents and the mob boss initially walked ahead calmly with his bodyguards in close proximity. The heavies lengthened their bird-like strides and hastily moved away from a huge barge that was berthed along the pier on Black Tom Island.

The three criminals quickly discarded their coats to release and display their huge wingspans, as they launched their muscular frames into the air. The agents followed in close pursuit along the wooden jetty and became frustrated at their inability to mimic their winged accomplices, as they dived off the fragile platform into the cold Hudson River. Within seconds, the barge full of TNT ammunition ignited behind them and a huge explosion sent shrapnel flying in every direction.

The Statue of Liberty was located nearby and the celebrated monument stood proud in seclusion on the remote islet of Liberty Island. The copper-skinned sculpture was damaged badly from the blast, as large pieces of metal were embedded into her green oxidised frame. The great symbol of justice maintained her majestic pose during the defenseless onslaught, as she was pounded with a shower of sharp debris. The majority of the flying waste from the major munitions depot hit the main body of the statue

10

but it was the torch at the end of her extended arm that received the most damage.

The city's fledgling Mafia leader was mesmerised by the catastrophic destruction caused by the explosion and evil glints of orange light reflected in his dark eyes from the fiery chaos that surrounded him. The youthful gangster stared in the opposite direction towards the Jersey Journal Building, as another piece of shrapnel bedded itself into the clock tower. The jagged piece of metal penetrated the clock face causing the hands to stop at exactly 02:12am.

The inexperienced Gullfather was called Don Brando Ceeguloni and the seagull menacingly shaped a raw smile across his curved yellow beak. His two magpie henchmen flew close by and provided an anthem of sinister laughter. The mobsters were totally oblivious to the devastating effect that their actions of sabotage were having on the outside world. As they circled above the Hudson River, the explosion was being replicated as a parallel devastation in a world where humans ruled.

New York City was now in great danger on both sides and the *Great Black-Backed Gull* had gained a real taste for anarchy. Since his recent arrival from the Mediterranean island of Sicily, upheaval and destruction was becoming common place in Manhattan.

The Black Tom explosion had achieved the desired effect and formed the first phase of the new Gullfather's master plan. The second stage of the task could now be implemented and the fledgling seagull was ready to begin a long construction campaign.

The preparations took a lengthy period to near completion and now it was time to lure a certain individual to the Gullfather's strange world. The heroic reputation of a young boy from the other side had alerted the attention of the Mafia boss. The boy possessed a coin that held the magic powers necessary to control the greatest weapon of all time. Don Brando Ceeguloni sensed it was now time to entice Bradley Baker to *his* chaotic world of unprecedented evil!

The Gullfather
of New York

2

The Twelfth Child

It was a humid Saturday night in Devon during the Easter break and the car park adjacent Sandmouth police headquarters was a hive of activity. A small detachment of uniformed officers were struggling to restrain a group of drunken revellers. The rowdy bunch of individuals had just disembarked from a convoy of six police vans and were now being ushered towards the concrete steps that fronted the main entrance to the station.

The majority of the disobedient factions were handcuffed and the remaining suspects had their arms hooked securely behind their backs, as the arresting officers frog-marched the accused in single file up the steps. The unruly crowd were led through the blue double-doors that fronted the police station's reception area, which was now filled to the brim with chanting party-goers.

An unwelcome stench tainted the air inside the lobby, as the smell of tobacco-stained clothing merged with alcohol-laden breath to create a stale aroma. The unregulated chorus of disruptive voices increased in volume, as each member was charged with *drunk and disorderly* behavior following their fracas outside a karaoke bar in the town centre.

Two flustered detectives pushed their way through the boisterous crowd and finally strode to safety behind the reception counter. The plain-clothed officers had seriously mistimed their arrival and they nodded in acknowledgement to the desk sergeant, who raised his eye-brows in disgust. Their presence at the station was totally unrelated to the pub episode and they were keen to gain access to one of the back offices to continue with their own inquiries. They were investigating a much more serious incident and they looked back at the inebriated group with distaste, as they waited patiently in front of an oak paneled door.

The first detective presented his security tag to the card reader and the latch clicked open in recognition, as the two officers pushed against the heavy door. Both men rushed forward and the door slammed shut behind them, as they ran towards a room at the end of the poorly lit corridor. The office contained the files they needed to access and add their latest piece of evidence to support an ongoing case into some missing children.

Once inside the room a light switch was flipped and the mesh-covered fluorescent tubes flickered until the internal starter bulb triggered the ceiling unit. The resulting light illuminated the dank office to reveal a grey-coloured filing cabinet in the far corner. The case file was retrieved and opened, as the older detective placed an unusually large feather onto a piece of paper.

"What's the significance of the feather?" asked the junior officer, as his senior colleague scratched his bald head and placed a strip of clear tape to secure the tip of a large black-coloured quill onto the paper.

Detective Inspector Sharp displayed an awkward frown, as he bit gently at his bottom lip to remove a stray piece of sticky tape. The puzzled officer shook his head and unbuttoned his shirt collar to loosen his tie, as he gasped. "That's better… still can't get used to wearing plain clothes - much preferred the uniform when I was a P.C."

"You should be proud of yourself… making detective inspector at your ripe old age – it's quite an achievement!" laughed the much younger officer.

"Less of the cheek, Gribbon… I'm not that old!" replied D.I. Sharp, as he carefully placed the paper onto the desk. "The promotion came as a bit of a shock… but I'm really pleased to have been recognized by the Chief Inspector of Sandmouth Police and being able to get stuck into real investigative work at last – although this latest case is very disturbing and a bit of a mystery!"

Detective Gribbon nodded in agreement and asked. "Well it's pretty close to home for you and quite relative to your own family situation… especially as most of the missing children are of a similar age to one of your nephew's - aren't they?"

"They sure are… the ages of the eleven kids that have vanished before tonight's incident ranged between ten and sixteen – and according the case file it can't be a coincidence that they are all recognized as *gifted and talented* pupils at their respective schools!" replied D.I. Sharp, as he pushed the file to one side and picked up a framed photograph of his sister's family. He rubbed his thumb over the face of the youngest Chilcott brother in the picture and his voice faltered slightly. "Musgrove is fifteen now… he's a brave young lad but he could so easily have been one of the missing kids too – he's also been recognized recently as a *gifted and talented* student at Sandmouth Secondary School!" He concluded and placed the photo frame next to the telephone on his desk, as he pulled a sealed plastic bag from his pocket that held a blue-coloured ribbon. "This is the thing that disturbs me most, though… I'm just hoping it doesn't belong to one of Musgrove's friends."

"That's the hair ribbon we found earlier this evening next to the feather at the base of the clock tower… who do you think it belongs too?" asked the young detective, as he flicked his dark fringe away from his eyes.

"There's only one local girl that I'm aware of that wears blue ribbons like these in her hair… a pretty little blonde thing with pig-tails and she also attends Sandmouth Secondary School," replied D.I. Sharp, as he scrunched the package in his clenched hand. "Her name is Sereny Ugbrooke… I spoke to her mother this morning and again about twenty minutes ago - she told me her daughter still hadn't arrived home!" He declared. "Sereny is also a friend of that Baker boy… you know - his parents bought the Haytor Hotel just before Christmas."

"Yeah, I know the family quite well… I helped them recently when a guest tried to steal some whiskey from their hotel bar - nice people, I think they moved down from Yorkshire didn't they?"

confirmed Detective Gribbon. "And their boy is called Bradley… there's something about him – can't quite put my finger on it!" He exclaimed. "And I believe his Aunt lives above Amley's Cove… about half a mile down the coastal road?"

"That's right… Vera Penworthy – an eccentric old lady but a pleasant chubby little woman all the same!" exclaimed D.I. Sharp. "I had to pay her a visit last summer when Musgrove and Bradley disappeared with the Ugbrooke girl… all three of them turned up safe in the end but I can't believe that Sereny may have disappeared again – and this time I fear the worst for her and the other eleven kids that have gone missing!" He continued. "It would make her the twelfth child to vanish in the last three weeks… we've got to get to the bottom of this mystery before the media get hold of the story and create unnecessary panic – the last thing we need is a scaremongering campaign spreading across Devon!"

"What do you suggest we do next?" asked the young officer, as his older partner closed the file and handed Detective Gribbon the blue ribbon. "Should we go back to the clock tower at the harbourside?"

"No... it's too dark," insisted D.I. Sharp, as he placed the case file back in the top drawer of the filing cabinet and locked the unit. "We'll go back down there tomorrow... there's a good chance we'll find more evidence in the light of day," he explained, as he rubbed his unshaven chin and then turned off the light. The two officers left the confines of the office and the detective inspector continued. "The huge size of that feather intrigues me... I've not come across anything like it before and I can't make out what type of bird it could possibly associate with – I suggest we get it across to forensics in the morning!"

The police officers walked down the corridor towards the lobby and the noise of the drunken crowd heightened again, as they neared the reception door. D.I. Sharp looked at his partner and flicked his head sideways to indicate that they abort their chosen route out of the station. "Tell you what... let's take the back entrance – can't stand the thought of mingling with that wayward lot out there again!"

"Good idea!" replied Detective Gribbon, as they turned and headed back down the narrow passageway. "So what time shall we meet up in the morning, Sir?"

"We won't be meeting up... well, not in the morning at least!" stated D.I. Sharp, as he pushed on the emergency release bar that spanned the width of the rear exit door. "Like I said... I'd like to get that feather down to forensics for an examination first thing – so if you could come in to deal with that and also get them to test the ribbon for DNA samples I'd appreciate it," he insisted. "It's the start of the Easter holidays, so whilst you're getting on with that... I'm going to catch up with my nephew and then pay a visit to the Haytor Hotel – I'm hoping that Musgrove and his friend Bradley Baker might be able to shed some light on young Sereny's possible disappearance!"

The emergency exit door closed slowly behind, as the two officers continued to chat. They walked out of the building towards the car park and agreed their tasks for the following day. The tired officers then said their farewells and climbed into their respective vehicles to drive away, as a strange figure emerged from the shadows.

The tall dark individual sniggered and placed his foot against the frame to prevent the door from locking, as he combed his stubby fingers through his thin black feathery hair. Then the intruder covertly squeezed his elongated body and neck through the gap, as his shirt caught on the latch. The unwelcome visitor unhooked his clothing and tucked his shirt tails back inside his trousers, as he made his way quietly along the corridor.

The prowler laughingly snorted to himself, as he heard the distant voice of the frustrated desk sergeant bellowing at the unruly crowd in the reception area. The chaotic noise created by the over-zealous drunks in the lobby continued to reverberate through the empty corridors of the police station, as the trespasser entered the detective's office. He prized open the drawer of the locked cabinet that contained the *missing children* case file. He then pulled out a compact digital camera from his jacket pocket and placed the device against his hook-tipped nose, as he focused a piercing eye through the lens. He swallowed nervously and his pale throat moved to compensate for a deep intake of breath, as he proceeded to take pictures of the file's sensitive contents. The stranger paused momentarily and looked out of the window to ensure his intrusion was still covert, as the light from the camera's flash bounced off the office walls.

D.I. Sharp was driving his car out of the car park and the flashing light from the camera caught his attention. The inquisitive policeman checked his rearview mirror and stopped the car immediately, as he turned his head to face the building. He assessed the office block but apart from the reception area all the windows in the building remained darkened. He shrugged his shoulders and muttered to himself, as rain drops started to appear on the windscreen. "It must have been a flash of lightning in the distance and it looks like the weather is about to turn... I'd better get home before we have a serious downpour."

The imposter peered through the vertical blinds and breathed a sigh of relief, as the car drove away. He had managed to avoid being discovered and was now in possession of some very useful information. His name was Marc Troon, posing as an unscrupulous reporter and freelance journalist working undercover for a public relations agency.

Tonight's discovery inside the Sandmouth police station would make for a great headline story and the imposter cackled to himself. "The editor of the local newspaper will pay good money for such a unique exclusive." Troon sniggered again and revelled in his scooping prowess at unearthing this mysterious seaside blockbuster, as he muttered. "And the Magpie's gonna love this... I can't think of a better way of weeding out *the eternal chosen one*!"

Apart from aiding and abetting his sinister accomplice, the publication of the story was bound to cause major embarrassment to the Sandmouth police. The intruder was looking forward to seeing his name accredited at the top of the editorial and he finished the deed by tidying the contents of the file. He placed them carefully back inside the filing cabinet and then made his way out of the building, as he placed the camera back inside his pocket. Troon sniggered again and then uttered, in a menacing tone. "Wait while the editor of the *Herald Express* gets a load of this information," he gloated and opened his telescopic umbrella to shield his fusty clothing from the heavy raindrops that were now pounding the tarmac. "I'd better get back to my hotel room pretty-pronto and get the press release emailed over to the newspaper before they turn off their printing presses... this stuff will make a brilliant headline for tomorrow's front page and will hopefully help lure the bait to the trap!"

of New York

3

Black and White

Patrick and Margaret Baker had settled in well to life as hoteliers in the picturesque seaside town of Sandmouth. Within three months of trading, the business had gone from strength to strength since they took ownership of the run-down Victorian villa just before Christmas. The Haytor Hotel was fully booked for the Bank Holiday period and the breakfast shift had just finished on the first Sunday morning during Easter.

Bradley walked into the kitchen carrying the last few plates from the dining room and placed them by the sink, as he wiped his brow. "I think the last few guests have gone out for the day and I'm sort of thinking it might be better being back at school... rather than serving customers their full English breakfasts!" He groaned and scraped a half-eaten sausage and what was left of a sticky egg yolk into the food recycle bin.

Margaret smiled at her handsome twelve year old son and thanked him for helping out in the kitchen. "Your father and I really appreciate your help, Bradley... I know it's the start of the school holidays but what with John and Pam both ringing in sick – it has left us a bit short-staffed to say the least."

"I don't really mind helping out, Mum... it beats math lessons any time!" he laughed and walked towards an entrance that led to the owner's accommodation. "Anyhow, speaking of staff... where is Dad?"

"Cheeky beggar!" laughed Margaret. "He's taken Frannie round to your Aunt Vera's... we thought it would be best for your little sister to sleep over there for a few days until we quietened down a bit – and she'll be able to keep Grandma Penworthy company too," replied Bradley's mother, as she picked up a tea towel and started to dry the remaining dishes. "So what are you up to today then?" she asked and placed the metal baking trays back in the bottom of the large oven. "Anything exciting planned?"

Bradley turned to face his inquisitive mother. "Muzzy said he might come over later and we were thinking of meeting up with Sereny… thought we might nip down to Amley's Cove and take K3 for a walk with us."

"That's sounds like a good plan!" replied Margaret, as the young Burnese Mountain Dog's ears pricked up from the basket in the corner of the adjoining room. There was nothing wrong with the puppy's hearing and the fluffy hound appeared in the doorway. "Speak of the devil… here he is - the little fella must have heard you!"

K3 was a surprise Christmas present from Bradley's parents. The puppy was a replacement for the original family Burnese Mountain Dog that died at the hands of the Shade Runner back in Ravenswood.

Unbeknown to Bradley's parents, K3 was a rejuvenated version of the deceased K2, who had sacrificed his life to help their son gain access to Pathylon. Now that the boy hero had returned safely, K2's soul had been released from the Vortex of Silvermoor and the dog had returned to his master in the form of a new puppy.

K3's tail wagged from side to side and he offered a paw to his young master. "Woof... woof!" he barked in a deep bellowing tone, as his pink tongue moved in and out with an excited rhythm to match his heavy panting.

Bradley reached down and whispered in the dog's ear. "It's okay, boy... we'll go for a walk when Muzzy gets here and I'm glad you've accepted your new name too – I couldn't really call you K2 again or it would have raised too much suspicion."

The dog broadened his mouth to simulate a smile and licked Bradley's ear, as he whispered back. "I understand... I don't care what you call me - I'm just glad to be back here safe with you and out of that ghostly pit beneath the old blue light in Ravenswood."

Bradley closed his eyes to enjoy the innocent smell of puppy-breath wafting under his nostrils, as he grinned. The comforting moment rekindled some fond memories before he reopened his eyes and called out to his mother. "I'm just gonna get changed out of these *black and white* clothes... fed up of looking like a Spanish waiter – some fella in the dining room called me *Manuel* from *Faulty Towers*!" he exclaimed and called the faithful dog into the owner's accommodation, as they made their way into his bedroom.

Margaret smiled, as the bedroom door slammed in the distance and she continued with her cleaning routine by wiping down the stainless steel worktops. Her concentration was interrupted by the sound of the front door bell ringing. "I wonder who that could be?" she muttered to herself. "Bradley said he thought all the guests had left for the day... better go and see who it is!" she exclaimed and quickly untied her pinny, as she left the confines of the commercial kitchen.

Bradley had also heard the sound of the bell, as he quickly got dressed into his familiar blue checked shirt and jeans then made his way into the reception area. K3 followed in close pursuit and they witnessed Margaret open the front door, as two male figures began to converse with her inside the entrance porch.

K3 barked again, as Bradley walked over to stand behind his mother. The boy peered inquisitively over her shoulder and recognized the two individuals immediately. "Muzzy!" he shouted. "What are you doing here… you're way too early!"

Musgrove glanced over to the other man, who was holding a rolled up newspaper in his left hand. K3 cowered away, as the stranger tapped the cylindrical weapon in the palm of his other hand. D.I. Sharp noticed the dog's discomfort and looked down at the worried animal, as he afforded the canine some reassurance by hiding the offending newspaper behind his brown trench coat. The young dog growled politely and decided to vacate the scene, as he disappeared down the hallway to trundle back to the safety of his basket.

"Why are you here, Detective?" asked Margaret. "Has something happened to Patrick and Frannie?"

"No…no, nothing of the sort, Mrs. Baker – and its errrr, Detective Inspector actually," replied the police officer. "I've just called in to see my sister and young nephew here but thought it best to pay Bradley a visit before he finds out the bad news after reading this!" he exclaimed and held out a copy of the local *Herald Express*. "We've just picked up this copy of the morning paper from the newsagents and it's hot off the press… some journalist must have broken into the police station last night and got access to one of my case files – this information should not have been made public at this stage of the investigation!"

Bradley stepped forward and held out his hand to retrieve the newspaper. D.I. Sharp obliged and handed it to the puzzled boy, as Musgrove held his head down. "What it is, Muzzy… have you already read it?" asked Bradley in a worried tone, as a noisy flock of seagulls flew in circles above the hotel.

"You're both making me very nervous… what's going on?"

Muzzy stayed silent, as the detective insisted that Bradley read the front page article. "I think it may involve one of your friends… the journalist certainly seems to think so from the content of his editorial – Sereny Ugbrooke still hasn't returned home and her mother is in pieces!"

Bradley's heart skipped a beat at the thought of something bad happening to Sereny. "I take it the rogue reporter you speak of is this *Marc Troon* chap?" he asked and straightened out the newspaper to check out who had written the article.

"Yes!" replied D.I. Sharp. "But don't worry, we have uniformed officers out looking for him… he will be arrested for breaking and entering police premises but there's nothing we can do about the information being made public – it's in print, so it's too late to do anything about it now!"

Bradley nodded and read out the headline. *"Twelfth child disappears near clock tower!"* He continued and read the rest of the article aloud so his mother could hear. *"Mystery deepens in Sandmouth. Police have stepped up their investigations into the disappearance of the latest missing child, who was last sighted walking near the famous 'clock tower' landmark in Sandmouth. The total number of missing children has now reached twelve and police are very suspicious that the incidents may be linked. All the youngsters have been recognised as Gifted & Talented pupils who attend local schools in the Devon area - last night witnesses spoke of a bird-like stranger dressed in a purple coat and hat, who was spotted talking to a young blonde-haired girl just before she vanished."*

Margaret pressed both hands against her face and puffed out her cheeks in a distressed manner. "That's terrible… all those poor children and their worried families – have you any idea where they could be?"

D.I. Sharp replied. "I'm afraid not… it's like all the kids have just vanished into thin air – the only thing we can link to each disappearance is the fact that they were all *gifted and talented* pupils at their respective schools!"

Bradley read the article again and corrected the detective. "Don't forget… there's another pretty obvious link to each incident - *Troon* mentions that all the missing children were last sighted near the clock tower down by the harbourside!"

Musgrove broke his silence and gently took the newspaper from his friend, as he folded it neatly. "According to my Uncle… everything written in this article is factual – apart from the bit on page two where the rogue journalist has assumed from my Uncle's notes that Sereny is the twelfth child to have been taken!"

D.I. Sharp nodded and confirmed. "Muzzy is right… the reporter looked at all the evidence in the case file and it's all there in *black and white* but he was wrong to publish our assumptions based on the blue ribbon we found near the clock tower last night – I'm still waiting for Detective Gribbon to text me with the DNA results from the forensics department!"

At that moment the police officer's mobile phone bleeped in his pocket and he retrieved the text message from his junior partner. "That's a coincidence... hopefully this is the results of the tests!" assumed D.I. Sharp, as he opened the message.

"What does it say?" asked Bradley in a nervous tone.

D.I. Sharp hesitated for a moment, as he read the message to himself. "It's mixed news... some good and as always I'm afraid there's some bad news too!"

Musgrove insisted that his uncle put them out of their misery and reveal the content of the text message. "Does the blue ribbon you found belong to Sereny or not?"

"No!" replied the detective inspector. "That's part of the good news... the other relates to the large black feather found near the clock tower with the ribbon – forensics couldn't confirm what type of bird the feather comes from so a specialist at *Living Coast Zoo* has agreed to take a look at it and Detective Gribbon is dropping off the sample to a Dr. Zoe Sparrow this afternoon!"

Bradley chuckled then exclaimed. "Now you're having us on... are you being serious – Dr. Sparrow the bird specialist?"

"That's what Detective Gribbon has just texted me!" confirmed D.I. Sharp.

Margaret nudged Bradley in the ribs and focussed the conversation back to the police officer's phone message. "So what's the bad news, D.I. Sharp?"

The senior detective afforded Bradley a stern look and concluded in a serious tone. "Well, as I was saying... just because the ribbon doesn't belong to Sereny Ugbrooke - we still have to locate her whereabouts and it could still infer that a twelfth child has disappeared, so I guess that's the bad news!"

Bradley disagreed and rushed out of the porch onto the gravel car park that fronted the hotel. "Not necessarily... there's no real proof that Sereny or even a twelfth child is actually missing and I've got an idea what may have happened – come with me!"

of New York

4

The High Priests Assemble

The rumble of deep thunder rolled ominously through the dark clouds above the arcane world of Pathylon. Intermittent bolts of lightning struck elevated landmarks all over the five regions including the newly built tower adjacent the Royal Palace in the city of Trad.

The King had called an urgent meeting to discuss another possible threat to the kingdom and all but one of the five regions were represented by the respective High Priests. With no representative from the Forest of Haldon present, delegates from the Blacklands, Devonia, Krogonia and the Galetis Empire convened inside the Royal Palace and they all waited for King Luccese to arrive.

An inquisitive conversation ensued, as Guan-yin, Henley, Grog and Meltor debated the recent upheaval that had resulted in Varuna and Flaglan's imprisonment in the tower. The High Priests continued to deliberate about the reason for their unscheduled summons to the palace, as their conversation was interrupted by a loud pounding on the private entrance to the chamber.

The senior members of the Royal Congress focussed their attention on the closed doors, as they began to open very slowly. A palace guard then stepped into the room and announced their monarch's arrival. "All stand for your King!"

The four High Priest's stood and a familiar dwarf entered the room, as Guan-yin chuckled. "Hi Turpol... hadn't heard about your new promotion!"

The dwarf ignored the Hartopian and walked ahead holding a strange object. The trusted Gatekeeper had been invited to attend the meeting to explain the relevance of the twisted piece of metal in his hand.

39

Turpol placed the distorted object on the table and stood next to Meltor, as he stared around the room to acknowledge the others.

An anthem of trumpets sounded, as Luccese finally entered the room and everyone clambered out of their seats to bow. The King saluted his High Priests and the eminent Gatekeeper, as he took his seat in the throne opposite the dwarf. "Please be seated everyone and thank you for attending this unscheduled gathering at such short notice," he announced and then explained. "The last time we met like this... our world was in great danger – although we won that battle, unfortunately I have to inform you that I believe we are again faced with yet another intimidating threat!"

The murmuring of shocked voices filled the room and Meltor asked for permission to speak. "Sire... surely our lands are now safe – Varuna and Flaglan are secured in the new tower, so any possible threat on our lands has surely been thwarted."

"You would think so, my dear friend... especially after such heroics from Henley's brave nephew – yet again we were forced to call upon the services of the *eternal chosen one* and Bradley Baker obliged by risking his life yet again to save our kingdom," replied Luccese. "The boy's encounter with the Shade Runner last time around was indeed a feat of true bravery... we are forever indebted to his final act of loyalty – I sincerely hope we do not have to call him back again!"

Grog grunted, as the Krogon cleared his throat and asked. "So please tell us, my lord... what or who threatens our world and what significance does that thing have?" he inquired, as everyone's attention was then drawn to the object brought in by the dwarf.

The King picked up the twisted metal cage and asked Turpol to explain, as the dwarf stood on his chair to address the delegates. "This damaged cage was found in the dessert beyond the Mountains that shield our lands... soon after Bradley Baker left us, I commissioned a team of scouts to enter the Unknown Land to make sure the Amulet of Silvermoor was still secured on Mount Pero."

Guan-yin interrupted. "But why did you feel the need to check on the jewel… the sapphire was safely returned just after Bradley Baker returned to his own world some time ago – surely the Amulet of Silvermoor poses no further threat to Pathylon!"

Turpol assured the young female Hartopian that the sapphire's location was not the reason for his concern. "Whilst exploring the area… the scouts ventured beyond the Peronto Alps and arrived at the Vortex of Silvermoor - they found this thing near the entrance to the time portal." Explained the dwarf, as he lifted the metal object and added. "The skeleton of a small bird-like creature was found inside the cage… I had the carcass removed so it did not cause any offence or discomfort to anyone – it was proof that someone in a world away from ours has been experimenting with some kind of weapon!"

Meltor asked. "What significance do you think the remains of the bird and the cage have?"

The dwarf continued. "The metal from which the cage is made derives from a place far beyond the Unknown Land… a place where all the people have been transformed into birds – a place that mirrors a great Metropolis in the outside world where Bradley Baker originates!"

King Luccese stopped Turpol to interject and revealed the reason why he had called the High Priests together, as he looked over to Meltor. "As I feared, we may yet again have to call on *the eternal chosen one* for help... we have reason to believe that the coin is not currently in your protégé's possession – the sacred grobite is vulnerable and if it falls into the wrong hands, Pathylon would be in great danger!"

Meltor concurred. "I agree with your concerns, my lord... but what does the twisted cage found by the scouts have to do with all this?"

Henley felt he had to say something, as he ran his fingers over the cold metal object. "I have come across this design before... it is a device used to imprison the mind," he stated and pulled the loose wires that hung from the cage. "I have visited the place you speak of... where this originates from and I've witnessed the results of a great explosion that produced the shrapnel to create this indestructible metal alloy."

Meltor, Guan-yin and Grog spoke simultaneously. "What is the name of this place?"

Henley, Turpol and King Luccese replied in unison. "New York!"

The King continued to discuss the implications of what Turpol and the others had discussed. "We know what this metal can be used for and as the Gatekeeper surmised... I agree that someone or something is definitely planning to make some kind of weapon out of it!" He declared.

Turpol concurred. "For the disfigured cage and skeleton to be found so close to the time portal entrance... it would indicate that some sort of high-powered weapon is being developed but has failed to reach Pathylon on this occasion – we need to act fast to prevent the next assault reaching our kingdom."

Henley made a suggestion. "Would you like me to return to New York and find out what's going on?"

The King hesitated for a moment. "No... it's too dangerous for you or any of the others present here

44

today to make that journey alone – I don't want to risk losing any important members of my Royal Congress!" He Insisted. "The vortex is very weak and so I have come up with a better idea!"

Grog enquired. "What do you have in mind, my lord?"

Luccese dismissed the Krogon and his fellow High Priests. "You must trust me to make the right decision, all will be revealed in due course!" declared Luccese and he brought the meeting to an abrupt conclusion, as the delegates began to leave the room. Luccese asked Turpol to stay behind and explained to the dwarf. "There is far too much at stake and I need the High Priests to stay focussed on the security of their own regions here in Pathylon, in case we are attacked… therefore, I need you to do something for me - you of all people will appreciate my reason because you have an unbiased view on this situation."

"Of course, your majesty… anything – what is it that you want me to do?" replied the Gatekeeper.

The King did not want to risk the chance of anyone hearing his next request so he leant down to whisper in the dwarf's large grey ear. "I know you intend to return to Crystal City to your home in Rekab tomorrow… but before you go – I need you to pay a visit to the tower and bring Flaglan back here."

"But, Sire… she is a traitor!" replied Turpol.

Luccese placed his hand over the Gatekeeper's mouth. "Shhhhhhh… I know what she is and what she has done to harm my authority in the past – time and time again she has plotted my downfall with Varuna." He agreed. "But I have an idea… please trust me, Turpol – I know what I'm doing!"

"Very well… my lord," replied the reluctant dwarf.

Meanwhile back in Sandmouth, Margaret insisted on staying behind in the hotel, as D.I. Sharp and his nephew followed Bradley down the hill towards the harbour. "Wait up, Bradley… you're running too fast!" shouted Musgrove and rolled up the newspaper again in his hands, as his uncle lagged further behind.

Bradley increased his pace until he reached a slight turn in the road and seized an opportunity to hide, as he jumped sideways over a privet hedge. He then opened a nearby gate and waited for the sound of Musgrove's footsteps to approach, as he reached out to grab his startled friend. The exhausted police officer carried on running down the hill and Bradley kept his hand over the teenager's mouth to stop him shouting until D.I. Sharp was out of earshot.

The disgruntled teenager wriggled free and glared at his friend. "What are you doing... you idiot – you nearly pulled my head off!"

"Shushhhh," laughed Bradley. "I had to lose the adults... I knew Mum couldn't leave the hotel and I needed your Uncle out of the way too."

"Why?" insisted Musgrove, as he straightened his hoody.

"This is why!" exclaimed Bradley and lifted his new mobile phone to show Musgrove a message on the screen. "Your Uncle wasn't the only one expecting a text message... this one has been sent to me from Jefferson Crabtree – he's in America!"

"What's the significance of this particular message?" asked Musgrove. "You get loads of texts from him... the guy is obsessed!"

"Jefferson is visiting New York during the Easter holidays with his parents... they are staying over there for two weeks to check things out - in readiness for a permanent move back to the States in the summer," explained Bradley, as he scrolled down the message to the important bit. "Do you remember when we arrived back home after our last adventure in Pathylon... and Jefferson kept hold of the sacred coin?"

"Yes... go on!" insisted the impatient teenager.

"Well... Jefferson messaged me about a week ago to inform me that the coin had started to vibrate again and you know what that means – don't you?" revealed the excited boy.

"Absolutely-dootly, Brad... me old mucker - another amazing adventure!" exclaimed Musgrove in an excited tone.

"You bet, Muzzy!" replied Bradley. "And take a look at the last text Jefferson sent me... he's duplicated the secret message that appeared around the edge of the grobite when it started to glow!"

"That's brilliant… read it out, Brad – the light is reflecting on the screen so I can't see it properly and the writing's too small!" insisted Musgrove.

Bradley proceeded to read out the new message that had appeared around the edge of the gold coin. *"Seek out a door that hides the golden girl and discover Black Tom by following the ancient path to the Gullfather of New York!"*

"What are you thinking?" asked Musgrove.

Bradley revealed his interpretation of the message. "Well for starters… remember what happened to Sereny inside the Pyramids of Blood during our last adventure – it reminds me of when she jumped into the pool of liquid gold, so I guess she must be the one that the message refers to as *the golden girl*!"

"Well, if Sereny is the golden girl… where is the door that she's supposed to be hiding behind and who is *Black Tom*?" asked Musgrove, as he stood up and arched his back.

Bradley edged his way back over to the hedge that bordered the garden, as he looked up and down the road to make sure the coast was clear. "Follow me,

Muzzy… we need to head down to the harbour - I've got a pretty good idea which door the message on the coin is referring to!"

"Wait!" shouted Musgrove. "What has *New York* and the *Gullfather* got to do with all this… it sounds a bit sinister and gangster-like, bit like an extract from an *Al Capone* movie, don't you think – maybe the *black* feather belongs to someone called *Tom* and it has something to do with the message too?"

"Obviously, *New York* is where Jefferson is holding the coin… so I guess we will have to follow some ancient path to reach him!" replied Bradley, as he increased his running pace. "As for the feather… maybe the bird-like stranger mentioned in the newspaper report has something to do with the mysterious disappearance of all those Devon school children – maybe he's called Tom?" panted Bradley, as the two boys continued to run down the hill. "Let's locate the door first… I've got a feeling that whatever lies behind it holds the answers to what we're looking for - so I'm sure we'll be able to work out the Gullfather, Black Tom and feather stuff later!"

5

Black Tom

A week earlier, Jefferson Crabtree had taken an authorized absence from school. The African-American boy and his parents had completed the long flight from London Heathrow and had arrived safely back in their native New York State.

The arrival at J.F.K. Airport was a distant memory, as the car hired for their two week stay approached a light-blue painted house on the corner of Main Street and Mountain Avenue. The Crabtree family home was located in the village of Highland Falls on the outskirts of Black Rock Forest near the Hudson River.

Highland Falls was located within the mid-Hudson Valley and just over an hour's drive from the busy Manhattan district where Jefferson's father used to work. Mr. Crabtree had managed to secure his old position as area manager within a New York real estate company. Both Charles and Marian were looking forward to refurnishing their old house in readiness for a move back to the states. The house was now empty following a rental families' departure and they had returned from England to prepare the property for their permanent move back to the States in the summer.

The familiar noise of hot rubber driving over loose gravel transmitted a welcome sound through the car's chassis, as the vehicle came to a halt on the driveway. Charles applied the handbrake before releasing the central locking and the three weary travelers got out of the car. Jefferson followed his father onto the front porch area, whilst his mother opened the front door to the house.

The twelve-year-old boy's sneakers screeched on the wooden floor as he flung out his arms and swirled on the spot in delight. "It's great to be home after two years in England... I'm really looking forward to meeting up with my old chums from Fort Montgomery Elementary – no doubt they'll all be attending *James O'Neill* High School now!"

Marian smiled at her son, as she entered the hallway and strode carefully over the thirty-or-so unopened envelopes that were strewn over the wooden floor. "I'm relieved you're pleased to be back, Jefferson... I know the majority of the village makeup is white but your African American and Hispanic friends will be pleased to see you again."

"Don't talk like that, Marian!" exclaimed Charles in an exhausted tone, as he put the heavy suitcases down by the telephone table. "You make it sound like Jefferson has never mixed with white kids... he got on just fine with his Rugby team mates at Maulby Grammar School - especially young Bradley Baker!"

Jefferson patted his father on the back and he winked in acknowledgment, in readiness to tease his naïve mother. "Dad's right, Mum... we're not living in the 1800's anymore - the valley may have been one of the major regions of conflict during the American Revolution but I'm pretty sure President Obama recently announced that Highland Falls had been fully liberated since then!"

Marian bent down and picked up a small pile of the large-sized envelopes, as she proceeded to smack her cheeky son playfully across the head with them. Jefferson's baseball-cap flew across the hallway like a flying saucer and rebounded against a wall mirror, as the startled boy's afro-length hair sprung outward. The irritated woman had fallen *hook-line and sinker* for his *leg-pulling* antics and she insisted on justifying her statistical comments about ethnic origin with an explanation. "You know I didn't mean it like that and I agree with everything your Father said... especially about Bradley and the rest of the Baker family – and I'll especially miss my coffee mornings with Margaret when we move over here permanently."

Charles and Jefferson put their arms around the tearful woman, as Mr. Crabtree consoled his wife. "Now don't you start getting upset again, Marian...

me and Jefferson were only winding you up," he reassured and nodded towards the kitchen door, as an indication to his son. "Please take the pint of milk we've just purchased from the village store and go put the kettle on, Jefferson... I think your Mum would appreciate a nice hot cup of English tea!"

Jefferson obliged and headed for the kitchen, as he felt a slight vibration against his leg. He put his hand inside his baggy-jeans pocket and placed his fingers around the warm metal disc. "The sacred coin is getting hot!" he exclaimed quietly. "That's impossible... I've been dreading this moment - I thought only Bradley Baker had the power to control the grobite!" he muttered and thought back to a conversation he had with Bradley's so-called uncle in Pathylon. "Bradley is supposed to be the eternal chosen one... not me – Henley Baker assured me that this wouldn't happen!"

Mr. and Mrs. Crabtree went back outside to finish unloading the car and soon returned to settle into the comfy seats in the main lounge. Jefferson's father shouted to enquire as to whether the tea was ready.

His confused son answered back knowing full well that he hadn't even filled the kettle with water. "Nearly ready, Dad... I'm waiting for the water to boil!" He fibbed and quickly ran the cold water tap. "Just looking for the sugar!"

The lounge TV's volume burst into sound and Jefferson flipped the switch to operate the kettle. The element started to heat up and the noise drowned out the sound of the television, as he removed the coin from his pocket. The excited boy began to read out the inscription around the edge. *"Seek out a door that hides the golden girl and discover Black Tom by following the ancient path to the Gullfather of New York!"*

Jefferson's concentration was interrupted by the kettle's thermostat tripping, as the switch clicked off. He began to pour the hot water over the tea bags and was startled, as his father suddenly appeared behind him. Charles spotted the grobite lying face down on the kitchen unit. "What have you got there, Son?"

"Oh, errrr... ermmmm – it's just on old coin Bradley Baker gave it to me as a leaving present," fibbed Jefferson, as he grabbed the coin and placed it back in his pocket. "Here's your tea… you take yours through to the lounge and I'll bring this one in for Mum," he insisted and picked up the other cup.

Mr. Crabtree felt he'd been hustled along and decided not to question his son about Bradley's apparent gift. It was obvious that Jefferson felt embarrassed by his intervention and he afforded him the benefit of the doubt by changing the subject. "So… what are you going to do now, Jefferson?"

"I think I'll head up to my room for a bit… I need to text Bradley and let him know we've arrived safely!" replied the anxious boy, who was eager to inform the real *eternal chosen one* about the message on the coin.

Marian thanked Jefferson for the cup of tea and invited her husband to sit down to watch the news. "Come on dear, take the weight off your feet and let's catch up on what's been happening in the good old *U.S. of A* since we've been in sweet little England!"

Jefferson took immediate advantage of his mother's request and left the confines of the lounge. He headed straight upstairs and secured himself in the privacy of his bedroom by locking his door. He removed the coin from his trouser pocket again and placed his mobile phone on the bed next to the grobite. "That's weird!" he exclaimed. "My phone is connected to the internet... it looks like it's been *streaming* online for ages – I must have accidentally pushed a button whilst it was in my pocket!"

The boy was correct in his assumption. His mobile device had been connected to Bradley Baker's phone for the past hour and that was how the coin had been activated. Somehow the sacred grobite had managed to communicate with the boy hero back in Sandmouth via the mobile satellite network.

Jefferson realized what had happen and he quickly disconnected the phone from the internet. "Do I tell Bradley about the message... or not?" he deliberated. "The hierarchy in Pathylon specifically told me not to allow Bradley's return to Pathylon without their prior knowledge... I just wish they'd told me why!" He thought, as the coin stopped glowing immediately and the message around its edge disappeared. He picked the coin back up off the bed and muttered to himself. "The coin must have been calling Bradley... there must be something serious going on - it would only react in extreme circumstances!" He declared. "Pathylon must be in some sort of danger and I can't betray my friend... I will have to break the promise I made to Henley and inform the eternal chosen one about the message!" he decided. "I must text Bradley and let him know what's just happened... this could be the start of another amazing adventure and I'm intrigued to know why *New York* appeared in the message!"

About an hour had passed and still no reply from Bradley. The battery indicator on Jefferson's phone was flashing red and the unit powered down automatically. The boy plugged in the phone's charger lead and left it on his bedside cabinet, as he made his way back downstairs to the lounge. His mother and father were still snuggled on the same sofa facing the television set and Jefferson sat down next to his father to ask him a question. "Dad?"

"Yes, Son," replied Charles.

"This maybe a daft question… but do you happen to know *what* or *who* Black Tom is?" enquired Jefferson, as he looked over to see his mother fast asleep.

"Why are you asking me that?" replied Charles, as he sat forward to face his son in an apprehensive manner.

Jefferson looked puzzled. "Have I upset you by asking the question?"

His father paused for a moment and answered. "No…no, it's just – I errrm wasn't expecting you to ever ask me that particular question," replied Charles, as he stood up and walked over to turn off the TV. "How do you know about Tom?" He whispered. "Tell you what, don't answer… let's go into the kitchen and talk about it in there – away from your Mum."

Jefferson followed his father into the hallway that led through to the kitchen. The boy pulled out a heavy wooden chair and sat down, as he placed his arms on the surface of the large farmhouse-style table. He waited for his father to fill a glass with water and then asked the question again. "So who is Black Tom?"

"Well, it sort of isn't a person... the term *'Black Tom'* originally referred to an island in New York Harbour - next to Liberty Island," explained Charles. "The island received its name from a local legend... another African American resident named Tom."

"So why did we just leave the room... why didn't you want Mum to hear what we were talking about?" asked the curious boy. "What has this Tom *bloke* got to do with her?"

"Your Mum still gets upset when we talk about the *Black Tom* incident... it has a lot to do with her side of the family!" replied Charles. "We agreed a long time ago not mention it again!"

"So why do you cringe every time I say the words *Black Tom*?" asked Jefferson.

"It was the name given to a major munitions depot for the northeast during World War One... American industries were free to sell their materials to any buyer back then, but the American's allies were the only possible customers," explained the knowledgeable real estate manager.

"Sorry, Dad… you're losing me – and how do you know all this stuff, anyhow?" asked the confused boy.

Charles explained that he had studied the event at college and continued his account of an explosion that took place on the Black Tom Island back in 1916. "It was an act of sabotage by enemy agents to prevent the material from being used by the Allies in World War One," he explained. "It was reported that on the night of the attack, two million pounds of ammunition was being stored at the depot… all awaiting eventual shipment to Europe – the Jersey City's Commissioner of Public Safety reported he had been told the barge containing the munitions had been tied up at Black Tom to avoid a twenty-five dollar towing charge!"

"Okay… enough about the intricate detail, Dad - what does this have to do with our family?" asked Jefferson.

Charles agreed to stop delving into the finer details about the story and replied. "The devastation caused by the explosion brought so much shame on our family for many years to follow… it was a terrible state of affairs."

"Why?" asked Jefferson.

Charles paused for a few seconds and placed his hand over his mouth, as he rubbed his face. "A guy called Frank Hague was the Commissioner of Public Safety and he blamed Great Grandpa Tom… your Mum's Grandfather - for causing the explosion!"

"So was the island named after Grandpa Tom?" enquired Jefferson.

"Not sure… as I said, the island received its name from a New York African American resident named Tom – so there's a good possibility that it could have been him," replied Charles and scratched his head. "Don't quote me on that bit though!"

"So why did this Frank Hague fella bring shame on our family?" asked Jefferson.

"The Commissioner of Public Safety initially blamed the incident on your Great Grandfather before admitting that it was really instigated by German agents who had sabotaged the Jersey City pier and

caused the explosion... but by then it was too late –
Great Grandpa Tom committed suicide a few months
later," explained Charles, as he topped-up his glass
with more water. "I guess it was just a case of being
in the wrong place at the wrong time!"

Jefferson watched his father drink the whole
contents of the glass before asking. "But why didn't
Great Grandpa Tom go to the police and tell them the
truth... why did he have to kill himself?"

"Back in those days, they wouldn't have believed
him... being a black African American didn't afford
you much of an advantage with the law – so he took
the honorable way out because he knew the
devastation caused by the blast would have sent him
to jail for a very long time," clarified his father. "As I
said, Black Tom Island used to lie in the Hudson
River not far from the Statue of Liberty... the
explosion caused $100,000 worth of damage to the
statue and back in those days that was a lot of money
– now it would amount to over two million dollars!"

"Wow, I can understand why Great Grandpa Tom
panicked... and I can see now why Mum gets a bit

64

funny about me hanging around with white kids – still it's no reason to be concerned," insisted Jefferson. "This happened such a long time ago!"

"You're right, Son… it's probably the reason why Mum gets a bit paranoid from time to time – but she's pretty much got over it now," said Charles. "I just didn't want her to hear us talking about it again… and I want you to promise me you won't mention this conversation in front of her!"

"I promise, but whilst we're on the subject… can you tell me more about what happened after the explosion to make Great Grandpa take his life?" asked Jefferson. "Surely the damage to the Statue of Liberty wasn't the only reason he committed suicide?"

"Okay, I'll try to remember what I read about the explosion when I was a college graduate… I know for sure that from then onward the torch in Liberty's hand was off limits to tourists," explained Charles. "Fragments from the explosion traveled long distances… some pieces lodged in the main body of the statue and some in the clock tower of the *Jersey*

Journal building in Jersey City - over a mile away!" his father continued. "The explosion was equivalent to an earthquake measuring between five and six on the *Richter* scale and was felt as far away as Philadelphia... windows broke as far as twenty five miles away, including thousands in lower Manhattan - even some window panes in Times Square were completely shattered!"

"That's incredible!" said Jefferson, as he began to imagine the devastating impact the explosion had on New York City.

"That's not all of it!" insisted Charles. "The Brooklyn Bridge was shaken... people as far away as Maryland were awakened by what they thought was an earthquake - property damage from the attack was estimated at $20 million, that's equivalent to about 425 million dollars in today's market!"

Jefferson reminded his father to stop including the full details of events as they happened. "You must have received a good set of marks for your graduation paper... but can you cut to the chase, Dad?"

Charles smiled and concluded his recollection of the incident. "The main reason why your Great Grandpa Tom killed himself was because he was one of the immigrants being processed at Ellis Island... like I said he just happened to be in the wrong place at the time of the incident. He and the other immigrants had to be evacuated to lower Manhattan. Reports vary, but as many as seven people may have been killed by the explosion, including; a Jersey City policeman, a Lehigh Valley Railroad Chief of Police, a ten week old infant and the barge captain!"

"No wonder the police didn't believe him back then... especially with losing two of their own men!" exclaimed Jefferson and then stayed silent, as his father got up from his seat. Charles walked towards the kitchen door and the grateful boy called over to thank his father for explaining about Black Tom. "Sorry for cutting you short a few times, Dad... I really appreciate you sharing that information with me - I promise not to say anything to Mum."

Charles sighed and responded. "No problem, Son... I'm amazed I can still recall the events so clearly –

and I forgot to ask, why did you want to know about Black Tom in the first place?"

Jefferson did not want to mention how the words Black Tom related to the message on the sacred coin so he quickly thought on his feet and used school homework as an excuse. "Don't worry, Dad... I won't write about Great Grandpa's suicide - I'll just keep the context of my essay to the bit about how the blast from the explosion damaged the Statue of Liberty!"

"Oh... okay – well, I better go and check on your Mum and you better start writing your essay before you forget what I just told you," insisted Charles. "I think my college notes are still in the bureau if you ever need more information about the event." He concluded and left the kitchen to return to the lounge

The boy was left to ponder the real meaning of Black Tom and how it could possibly relate to the message on the coin. His father had failed to mention a crucial point about another strange occurrence relating to the explosion back in 1916. The police witness reports had also mentioned three accomplices dressed in overcoats running away from the scene and taking to the skies like birds. This was crucial information surrounding the Black Tom explosion but for now it remained an enigma to Jefferson, who rushed back upstairs to retrieve the grobite from his bed. The message was still absent from the edge of the coin and he muttered to himself. "I've got an idea, how to get this thing glowing again... I'll need to get back in touch with Bradley once my phone has charged – hopefully by linking up with his mobile again, the coin will activate and lead me to more clues so I can start to unravel this weird mystery!"

6

Gus the Gargoyle

Back in Sandmouth, D.I. Sharp had given up looking for the two boys and he parked his unmarked police car in front of the station. The detective inspector proceeded to walk into the building to reconsult with his case notes, as he dialed his mobile to call Mrs. Baker at the Haytor Hotel to inform Margaret that her son and his nephew had eluded him.

The amused woman played down the officer's concerns and put it down to childish antics. "They've probably taken it upon themselves to go off and look for Sereny on their own... you know what they're like at that age – don't worry, I'll call you if I hear anything."

D.I. Sharp thanked Bradley's mother, as he marched across the reception area of the station. He made his way through to the back offices, where his fellow detective welcomed him and placed a copy of the newspaper on the deck. "I take it you've seen this?" asked Detective Gribbon.

"Yes... I've just got back from the Haytor Hotel – I informed Bradley Baker about it but he ran off with my nephew," remarked D.I. sharp, as he picked up the handset on his desktop telephone. "The boy said he had an idea about Sereny Ugbrooke but they headed off towards the harbour... I chased after them but couldn't keep up - I lost them as they were running down the hill from the hotel!"

"You need to get down to the gym and firm up that beer belly of yours!" joked Detective Gribbon, as his partner afforded him a disapproving look. "No, seriously... why do you think they ran off like that?" he asked.

"Not sure… but it's like Mrs. Baker said – they do childish stuff like that at their age!" chastised D.I. Sharpe. "Anyhow, let's not worry too much what the boys are up to… we've got an investigation to follow – I'm calling that Sparrow woman!" he insisted and proceeded to dial the number for Living Coast Zoo. "Hopefully the nice ornithologist lady will give us some clues about the black feather you left with her earlier this morning!"

Detective Gribbon paid his senior partner a compliment. "I'm impressed, Sir… that's a big word for a Sunday morning - ornithologist!"

"Very funny… well not that funny – not too impressed that we're in here working on the day of the Sabbath," replied D.I. Sharp, as he waited for the phone to connect. "My wife is not very happy that I'm going to miss church and yet another Sunday lunch… still – finding those missing school children is our priority and the whereabouts of the Ugbrooke girl is proving to be a real mystery to solve!"

Meanwhile, Bradley Baker and Musgrove Chilcott hid patiently behind a public telephone box across from the memorial clock tower near the harbour. The monument stood at the centre of a roundabout and they waited for an opportunity to cross the busy road to check out Bradley's notion about the door in the message.

A flock of hungry seagulls bombarded the nearby pavement, as they flew down to scavenge the contents of a discarded bag of chips. Musgrove raised his voice slightly to counter their constant screeching. "Blumming nuisance those gulls... anyhow, what makes you think that the door at the base of the clock tower has something to do with the clue on the coin?" asked Musgrove, as they edged nearer the curbside.

Bradley waved his arms to disperse the annoying birds and they flew towards the rooftops of a nearby building. The seagulls landed next to a pair of stone gargoyles and continued their annoying chatter, as the boy noticed one of the statues move its arm. "You're not going to believe what I just saw!" he exclaimed and nudged Musgrove. "See that weird-looking gargoyle up on the roof of the night club… I swear it just moved!"

Musgrove afforded his friend a disbelieving look and chuckled. "I think you're losing it, mate… all this Gullfather stuff mentioned on the coin is making you delusional – it was most likely one of those irritating seagulls flapping its wings!"

"Well you can stay here if you want," insisted Bradley. "But I'm going to check it out… you should know by now – anything is possible during our amazing adventures!"

Musgrove raised his eyebrows and reluctantly followed after his friend, as they headed up a small walkway that led to the back of the building. A metal fire escape spiraled up to the roof and it didn't take the inquisitive boys long to reach the top.

Bradley moved hesitantly towards the edge of the roof that overlooked the main road and spotted the two statues. The eternal chosen one climbed onto the balustrade façade and started to crawl along the thin ledge. He approached the first gargoyle and touched its head. "The stone feels very cold and it's quite clammy... this thing can't have moved – it's rock-hard!"

"I said you were losing it... now be careful not fall over the edge, Brad – get back over here!" warned Musgrove, as he watched from the side and held onto the crumbling brickwork of a tall chimney.

Bradley maneuvered his body in front of the small statue and began to examine the arm that he thought had moved. The limb was solid and the boy looked puzzled, as he called over to Musgrove. "I guess you were right, Muzzy... the coin's recent activity must be making me delusional!"

Suddenly the gargoyle's eyelids opened and two blood-red lights emitted from the statue's face like tiny laser beams. Bradley coiled back and slipped over the edge of the building, as he held out his hand to catch hold of the gargoyle's foot. Musgrove watched helplessly from the side in horror, as the boy hero pulled himself back up to face the stone figure again.

"Hello, Bradley Baker!" the diminutive statue croaked. "We've been expecting you!"

Musgrove stood open-mouthed and clung more tightly to the side of the chimney, as Bradley replied. "Did you just say… *we've* been expecting you?"

"Yes me and my twin brother over there!" explained the gargoyle, as he turned his head to create a grating sound and faced the other small statue. "That's Guy and my name is Gus… only one of us can wake up at any one time – so it's my turn today!"

Bradley waved his arm to summon Musgrove to join him but the frightened boy hesitated and shouted. "Are they friend or foe?"

"This one seems friendly enough!" replied Bradley. "Come over and listen to what he has to say!"

Musgrove tentatively joined his friend and they both sat on the ledge, as the gargoyle explained why he had woken. Gus told the boys that a flock of seagulls had just perched on the same ledge a few minutes ago and their squawking had revealed some important information. "I am right in assuming… you are the eternal chosen one – the famous Bradley Baker?"

Bradley was taken back. "Not sure about the famous bit… but yes I am Bradley Baker – how do you know my name?"

"My brother and I have been taking it in turns to watch you for quite a while… since your move from Ravenswood to Sandmouth before Christmas," replied Gus. "My cousin at the top of the cenotaph across from your old house in Yorkshire informed us that you were moving down here … in fact our distant cousins in New York City have also alerted us of more recent events."

"I always wondered what that weird looking statue was doing there above the blue light… now I know – this is crazy!" exclaimed Bradley. "I can't believe I'm talking to a stone figure on top of a night club in Sandmouth… and you mentioned New York!"

The gargoyle insisted that the boys listen to what he had to say. "I don't have much time… me and my brother only waken for short periods so here's what the seagulls said about the coin!"

"My coin… the sacred grobite?" exclaimed Bradley.

"Yes… the same coin that has revealed a message about the Gullfather of New York – make sure he doesn't attain its magic powers for his new weapon!"

Musgrove asked. "Why?"

The gargoyle did not reply and the reddened glow in its eyes diminished, as Bradley prodded the stone statue. "It's gone back to sleep… I can't believe it – now what do we do, Muzzy?"

Musgrove moved to one side to allow his friend to pass. "Well there's no point staying up here, Brad… I suggest we head back to the clock tower – that's if you still feel that the door at the base of the monument could have something to do with the message on the coin!"

"Absolutely!" replied Bradley. "I still believe the golden girl is hiding behind that door!" he presumed and scurried over the tiled roof to reach the top of the fire escape. "Let's get back down there… at least we know that the Gullfather exists and he wants to get his grubby hands on the coin to power some kind of weapon – we'll need to be extra vigilant from now on!"

7

A Clock Tower Riddle

The encounter with the gargoyle had provided Bradley and Musgrove with some very useful information about the importance of the coin in this particular adventure. The two boys knew they had to protect the sacred grobite at all costs and they repositioned themselves back behind the telephone box across from the roundabout near the harbour.

Bradley pointed to the base of the clock tower. "I've still got a strong feeling that the golden girl is behind that door... after all - it's the place where D.I. Sharp found the blue ribbon and the feather!"

Musgrove noticed a brass commemorative plate attached to one of the three sides of the monument. "I've always wondered what is written on that plaque... I'm going to check it out when we get over there – if that's okay with you?"

"Sure, no problem!" replied Bradley "But never mind about that for now... take a look over there - can you see that piece of paper sticking out from the bottom of the door?"

"Oh yeah... well spotted, Brad – let's get across and find out what's written on it!" replied Musgrove, as a safe gap appeared in the traffic and they both crossed the road.

The harbour was so busy with Easter holidaymakers that no-one really paid any attention to the boys. The clock tower stood proud at the centre of the roundabout and they walked casually around the base of the monument. Musgrove headed straight for the plaque and read out the words engraved on the brass plate; *"In testimony to the life and public services of Richard Mallock of Cockington Court Esquire."*

Bradley nodded to acknowledge Musgrove's inquisitive narration. "Interesting," he sighed and then looked around to make sure none of the pedestrians were watching their investigative work. He bent down to pull the piece of paper from the base of the door. "It looks like a note and it's tied up with another blue ribbon… just like Sereny's - let's see what it says!" he exclaimed and unravelled the scroll.

"Anything interesting?" asked Musgrove in an impatient tone, as he moved away from the plaque towards his friend.

Bradley finished reading the unusual message and revealed. "We need to work it out!"

"Work what out!" shouted Musgrove, as the sound of a passing open-topped tour bus drowned out his voice.

"It's addressed to me and it looks like a riddle… there's a scratchy signature at the bottom too - it's been signed by *the Magpie*!" replied Bradley. "Do you remember what the newspaper report said… this must be from the bird-like stranger spotted by witnesses – the one wearing the purple coat and hat?"

Musgrove scratched his head and then rubbed his fingers through his long blonde fringe to flick his hair from his eyes. "How would this so-called *Magpie* know you and why leave you a riddle?"

"I think he's trying to taunt me... it's as if this strange *Magpie* character has lured me to this place for a reason – the message around the coin wasn't meant for Jefferson, after all!" announced the eternal chosen one. "It was meant for me!"

"Read out the riddle then, Brad," asked Musgrove, as they ran away from the clock tower and back across the road to avoid any suspicious glances from passers-by.

Bradley unrolled the piece of paper again and began to recite the words on the scroll;

"For the eyes of the Eternal Chosen One. To find the ancient path... push on the lock when the hands of the clock match Black Tom day. Signed, the Magpie"

"The note mention's Black Tom again... the same as the message on the coin!" exclaimed Musgrove, as Bradley pulled out his mobile phone and started to make a call. "Who are you ringing?"

"Jefferson!" replied Bradley.

"But he's in New York!" cried Musgrove, as he pointed to the clock face on the tower. "They're about five hours behind us… it's just gone midday here so it's only seven o'clock over there – why don't you just check *google*?" he suggested. "You're bound to find the info about Black Tom online!"

Bradley checked the network signal on his phone. "No good… I haven't got a network signal - we must be in a bad reception area," he explained and shrugged his shoulders. "Oh, what the eck… I'll just call him - he's bound to be up and about!" insisted Bradley. "His body clock will still be in school mode… if he's anything like me!" laughed Bradley, as the international dialing tone led to a familiar voice sounding in his ear. "Hi… Jeffers – is that you?"

Jefferson sounded surprised to hear his English friend's voice. "Hey… how you doing, Bradley – did you get my text?"

"Sure did… that's amazing how the coin reacted that way – it's going to be very useful to know that we can control it using the mobile network!" replied

Bradley and informed his American friend about the riddle. "I need to ask you a question about Black Tom!"

"No problem, Bradley... it's funny you should ask – my Dad told me all about its history!" explained Jefferson. "He studied the subject in college... Black Tom was a small island near the Statue of Liberty that was destroyed by German secret agents back in 1916... there was a massive explosion and the..."

Bradley interrupted his informative friend. "Thanks Jeffers, sorry to butt in but you just hinted at some information we urgently need this end... we think Sereny is trapped behind a door beneath a clock tower here in Sandmouth – it's a long story but can you tell me the date of the Black Tom explosion?"

Jefferson paused. "I know the year, but Dad didn't mention anything about what the actual day and month was when it happened... wait there – I'll just check something!"

"Don't worry, we're not going anywhere... but please be quick – this phone call is costing me a fortune!" explained Bradley and laughed in a joking manner.

"Okay, I understand," replied Jefferson and then suggested that Bradley terminate the call whilst he ventured off to refer to his father's college notes that were in a writing bureau downstairs. "I'll text you with the day and month in about two minutes... then you can call me back when you've found Sereny and let me know she is safe and sound – is that okay?"

"Sounds good to me, Jeffers... don't be too long though – we look like a couple of *buskers* by the side of this roundabout and people will start handing over their money if we're lucky!" chuckled Bradley, as he touched the red *'end'* icon on the display screen of his new iPhone.

Musgrove commented. "Nice to see you've been entrusted with the latest mobile technology again!"

"Yeah... I'll try not to lose this one – I don't anticipate jumping into any more ice-clouds for a long time to come, that's for sure!" replied Bradley, as he looked over to the base of the clock tower again and muttered a desperate plea to himself. "I hope you're behind that door, Sereny… I'm beginning to get worried and I really miss you!"

Musgrove nudged his friend and quipped. "Wow… that was quick – you've got a text from our new secret agent in America!"

Bradley quickly snapped out of his personal thoughts and acknowledged Musgrove's joke, as he opened the text message from Jefferson. "*July 30th!*" he stated and opened the note containing the Magpie's riddle to remind himself of the content. "*Release the golden girl by pushing on the lock when the hands of the clock match Black Tom day!*"

Musgrove sighed. "Why do we always have to work out these stupid messages… why can't these villains just make it easy for us and write their cunning plans down in simple English?"

Bradley laughed and patted his friend on the shoulder. "Now… that wouldn't be much fun - would it?" he teased and insisted that they cross the road again to reach the centre of the roundabout. "Let's get over there… I think I've worked out the riddle!"

"Mr. bloody clever-clogs… how do you do it?" retorted Musgrove, as they ran over to the base of the clock tower. "So how do we match Black Tom day with the hands of the clock?"

"Easy… in the states, they always address their months before their days on electronic calendars – so that makes July the seventh month before the number thirty!" explained Bradley.

"What has that got to do with the hands on the clock?" asked Musgrove.

"We have to use the date as the time… 7:30am!" replied Bradley, as he looked up at one of the three clocks faces that adorned each side of the trilateral monument.

Musgrove followed his friend's line of sight and commented on the time. "We're too late then… it's coming up to 12:28 – it's nearly half past twelve!"

Bradley afforded his friend a smug look. "Not in New York it isn't!"

"What do you mean?" asked Musgrove, as a puzzled look spread across his face.

"Like you said… they are five hours behind us and Jefferson informed us that the Black Tom explosion happened in New York back in 1916!" explained Bradley. "So if we apply the time difference and follow the words in the riddle… we need to push the lock when the hands of the clock match Black Tom day – which in our time is 12:30!"

"You're either a genius or an absolute nutter!" shouted Musgrove, as they both placed their hands on the lock beneath the handle on the door. "I make it about thirty seconds before the hands on the clock reach the half hour mark!"

Musgrove's estimation was spot on and as the minute hand passed over the sixth Roman numeral, the boys pushed hard on the lock.

"Nothing's happening!" shouted Musgrove. "I'm pushing as hard as I can but it's not budging!"

"We must have missed something!" gasped Bradley.

"You've probably got the month and day the wrong way round!" exclaimed the frustrated teenager.

Bradley responded by correcting his friend. "There's no such time at seven minutes past thirty, you idiot… there has to be something obvious we've overlooked!" he cried and remembered the brass plate. "Ahhh… I wonder - what was the name of that chap on the plaque you read out a few minutes ago?"

Musgrove scrunched his nose and hunched his shoulders. "I can't remember… you didn't seem to be that interested – Richard somebody or other!"

"Wait there and keep your weight against the latch!" insisted Bradley, as he moved away from the door.

"Where are you going?" asked Musgrove.

"To check the commemorative plate on the other side… I think the guys surname name was *Mallock* and we may be pushing against the wrong lock!" explained Bradley, as Musgrove insisted he hurry before the minute hands on all three of the tower's clocks moved on to the next marker.

Bradley stood in front of the plaque and he repeated the inscription; "*In testimony to the life and public services of Richard Mallock of Cockington Court*

Esquire… I was right the name on the plaque is *Mal-lock* – this is it, this has to be the *lock* we're looking for!*"*

Musgrove shouted in a desperate tone. "Well push the damn thing then!"

Bradley obliged and placed the palm of his hand against the end of the surname and pushed just as the minute hand moved away from the half hour mark. "Anything happened?" He asked, as the door flung open and Musgrove's weight carried him head first into the base of the clock tower.

"You could say that!" replied Musgrove in a muffled voice, as he lifted his face from a pile of sand-filled hessian sacks.

Bradley rushed round to the open doorway and glanced across the road at a crowd of interested onlookers. "We've got an audience!"

Musgrove lifted his lanky frame out of the sand-bags and brushed the dust off his clothes, as he rose to his feet. "Well they can stare as long as they like but they'll be very disappointed… there's no sign of an ancient path or our *golden girl* in here - Sereny Ugbrooke isn't behind this particular door!"

Bradley stood open-mouthed with a closed fist against his hip and the tight fingers of his other hand clenched his ruffled hair. He moved away from the doorway and spoke softly. "I guess we need to search for another door... I was so certain this was the one – where next, Muzzy?"

Musgrove shrugged his shoulders and began to close the door. "Might as well lock this thing back up then!"

Bradley held out his arm and shouted. "Noooo... stop – leave the door ajar!" he suggested. "The riddle was left here by the Magpie for a reason... I still think we have missed something – let's wait over there for a bit so we don't attract any unnecessary attention to ourselves!"

Musgrove nodded and the two beleaguered boys made their way across the road and sat down on the pavement next to the telephone box again, as they contemplated their next move.

of New York

8

A Secret Aviary

The sail-like netting that secured the sea-birds inside the aviary at *Living Coast Zoo* blew gently in the breeze, as the tall angled masts withstood the strain. The familiar Sandmouth landmark was set into the cliffside overlooking the bay and contained an array of endangered species from across the world.

The aquatic conservation centre boasted many mammals and sea birds, including rare varieties of seals and penguins that swam openly in specially-designed naturalistic habitats. The architectural design of the outdoor and indoor exhibits nestled perfectly under the main enclosure. A series of private workshops and store rooms were located deep below the seawater pools; out of bounds to the general public and connected via a network of brightly coloured corridors depicting the various animals resident at the zoo.

Inside one of the clinically-painted white rooms in the basement, a beautiful voluptuous woman peered into a microscope that was part of an impressive range of equipment. Dr. Zoe Sparrow was working inside her laboratory and her slim hour-glass body was barely disguised by the white medical cloak she was wearing. Her hair was tied back in a bun and she wore a pair of black-rimmed designer spectacles that perched on the end of her turned-up nose. The lighting inside the room reflected against her bright red lipstick, as she held aloft a sample glass tile from her microscope.

The woman portrayed the look of a legal secretary and her long slender legs stretched elegantly down, as she sat straight-backed on the edge of a tall stool. The work being carried out by the new resident ornithologist was thought to be very important. Her supposed knowledge of the exotic birds in the zoo would be passed on to many thousands of people that visited the town's seafront attraction each year.

A large black feather was secured inside a clear plastic bag next to the microscope and it shifted slightly, as the door of the brightly lit room opened. Dr. Sparrow looked up and welcomed her two expected guests. "That was a quick journey, gentlemen... you must have driven very fast to get here from the police station so soon," she commented, as the detectives entered the laboratory.

"Thank you for agreeing to see us... especially on such a popular Sunday at the zoo – there's quite a queue gathering at the turnstiles and the sea lions inside the main enclosure are attracting a nice crowd," remarked D.I. Sharp in a nervous tone, as he made polite conversation and proceeded to remove his trench coat. The smitten officer then placed it on the back of a white plastic chair and continued to converse in an affectionate tone. "And it looked like you were busy when we came in... I hope my fellow officer and I are not interrupting anything but I did notice the feather from our case file in the plastic bag – I was wondering if you'd had a chance to examine it yet?"

The entrancing woman smiled and her eyes sparkled, as the two men's faces reacted by turning a slight shade of red. Dr. Sparrow's beauty was evident and the detectives were wary of her magnetic charm. She courteously invited Detective Gribbon to remove his jacket too and spoke softly to his balding partner, whose shiny head had developed a deep pink hue. "Please take a seat, Detective Inspector and make yourself comfortable… I have the results of the tests you've been waiting for – and they make for interesting reading."

D.I. Sharp could feel a bead of sweat rolling down the side of his face and he reached into his pocket to retrieve a white handkerchief. He proceeded to dab the cotton against his reddened skin to absorb his perspiring brow, as Dr. Sparrow acknowledged the nervous officer with a wry smile. The two detectives sat back and listened to the fictitious bird specialist, as the movement of her sultry lips caused their concentration to waiver every so often. The woman's allure was powerful and she started to explain the strange significance of the black feather's presence in Sandmouth. "This is no ordinary feather and it belongs to no ordinary bird!"

D.I. Sharp asked. "Are you able to tell us what type of bird it belongs too?"

"Of course… it is a tail feather from a *Magpie*!" announced Dr. Sparrow. "However, it's not a species of the bird that exists in your world… but I guess that is obvious by the sheer size of the feather!"

"Our *world*… do you mean Sandmouth or maybe even Devon?" enquired Detective Gribbon in an unsure tone.

Dr. Sparrow smiled again affectionately. "No… I mean *your world*!" she repeated and slid elegantly off the stool and reached over to pick up the plastic bag. The confident female removed the feather and held it in front of the police officer's face. "This belongs to a creature from a parallel world far away from the one you reside in… it originates from a villainous henchman employed by the *Gullfather of New York* – and he seeks a boy you both know quite well!"

"Who is this boy you speak of?" asked Detective Gribbon.

Dr. Sparrow hesitated, as she carefully placed the feather back inside the bag and replied. "A boy called *Bradley Baker*… and the Magpie also seeks a sacred gold coin beholden to the eternal chosen one – the coin contains great powers and is wanted desperately by the Gullfather!"

D.I. Sharp stood out of his seat and approached the strange woman. He noticed the tips of her ears pointing out slightly from her tied back hair. "What are you going on about… you're no ornithologist - who the hell are you and why are you wasting our time with all this talk of *Magpies* from other worlds and a so-called *Gullfather* of New York?"

"Do not underestimate the *so-called* Gullfather… he was once a fledgling seagull that had fled the scene of the Black Tom explosion in 1916 but he is now some forty years older!" warned Dr. Sparrow. "He has matured into a huge Great Black-Backed

Gull and this particular species are the largest and most impressive of the gulls... he stands proud amongst the mixed flocks that inhabit New York - therefore he is the only one of his kind and rules with an iron fist over his mobster gangs!" The sultry female concluded and then pulled the tie-back out of her hair, as her brown wavy locks flowed down over her petite shoulders. She removed her white coat to reveal her scantily-clad body, which was adorned with a flowing medieval costume made from the finest silk. "I think it is time I introduced myself properly!" she laughed. "My name is Flaglan and I am a High Priestess from the *Forest of Haldon* in a world called *Pathylon*... I have been sent here by my King to help you defeat the *Gullfather*!"

Detective Gribbon rose from his chair and both policemen took a step backwards. They looked shocked and confused, as Flaglan moved forward to explain her presence in the outside world.

D.I. Sharp afforded a disbelieving glance to his partner and suggested. "This has to be a joke... the *Gullfather*, an explosion in *1916* and now a *High*

Priestess - the lads back at the station must have set this up!" he laughed and stared into the bewitching eyes of the sorceress. "Are you a stripper-gram or something?"

Flaglan pitched her head back to reveal her slender neck and screeched softly. "No I'm not... now please re-take your seats, gentlemen – this could take a while, as I have lots more to tell you."

The High Priestess confirmed that she was working as an undercover agent at the zoo and she explained that she had been sent to the outside world by her King. Luccese had pardoned her for her recent treasonous behavior on the proviso that she completed a mission to find Bradley Baker and protect the sacred coin from falling into the wrong hands. She explained to the stunned detectives that D.I. Sharp had actually travelled to Pathylon during a previous adventure but his mind had since been erased by the power of the coin to protect Pathylon and Bradley Baker's real identity. She explained that the boy was the *eternal chosen one*, who had travelled through time to help save her world on numerous occasions. After repeating the information about Pathylon for a second time, the Tree Elf had finally convinced the police officers that she was telling the truth by revealing her pointed ears.

Flaglan perched her bottom on the edge of the stool to allow the two men some time to digest her amazing account of events, as D.I. Sharp spoke nervously. "So why are you telling us all this... why risk us finding out about Pathylon and reveal the Baker boy's identity, as well as jeopardize his unique ability to travel through time using a gold coin - what can we possibly do to help you and your people?"

The sorceress continued to explain the reason why she had been sent to the outside world. "The network of vortexes that allow time travel in and out of Pathylon have been weakened... during his last adventure, Bradley Baker was involved in a fracas inside the vortex that links Sandmouth to the Forbidden Caves."

Detective Gribbon interrupted. "Where are these Forbidden Caves you speak of?"

Flaglan continued. "The Forbidden Caves are situated inside the Forest of Haldon... one of the five regions in Pathylon of which I am a High Priestess – Bradley Baker fought an evil Shade Runner called Ethan Darke inside the vortex and now the main time portal linking our two worlds has been severely damaged," she explained. "Other time portals that link our worlds to New York have also been affected and we don't have long before they close... the vortex I travelled through was badly damaged!"

"What so how did you manage to get here and why were you the one they decided to send to our world?" asked D.I. Sharp.

"King Luccese and Meltor sent me because of my slight frame... the vortex was strong enough to allow my journey to your world and I was able to get here before the corridor of time finally imploded," replied the sorceress. "Unfortunately, this means there is no way back to Pathylon from here... and that brings me to the reason why I need your help."

"Go on... we're listening, Dr. Sparrow – I err mean, Flaglan!" replied D.I. Sharp, as the High

Priestess moved over to a large white door at the far end of the room.

"The girl you are searching for is waiting behind this doorway!" exclaimed Flaglan.

Detective Gribbon approached the Tree Elf and smiled, as he assumed the identity of the girl. "You must be referring to Sereny Ugbrooke."

Flaglan reciprocated the officer's smile and wrapped her slender fingers around the door handle. "Yes… Sereny Ugbrooke - known in Pathylon as the *golden girl*!"

D.I. Sharp asked. "Well… are you going to open the door?"

"Of course… but please understand that Sereny is aware of the situation and is also keen to help us," explained Flaglan and gripped the handle tightly, as the police officer's eyes lit up. "I know you have been searching for her but she has managed to play an important role in our mission by amassing reinforcements from across Sandmouth's harbourside and seafront – her help has been invaluable and has strengthened our campaign considerably."

"I'm glad to hear the Ugbrooke girl is safe... but what are the reinforcements you speak of – and what campaign are you referring to?" asked D.I. Sharp, as the High Priestess finally turned the handle.

"Captain Sharp and Lieutenant Gribbon... may I introduce you to your new police squad!" announced the sorceress, as she opened the door to reveal a secret aviary containing thousands of excited pigeons. "This is an army of police officers... at your command and reporting for duty!"

"Captain Sharp?" exclaimed detective Gribbon. "And you reckon I'm now a lieutenant... what's going on and where's Sereny Ugbrooke?"

9

The Pigeon Police

Marc Troon gathered his personal belongings, as he made his way out of the lift and into the huge open lobby of the lavishly decorated *Imperial Hotel*. He tipped the end of his hat to cover his unusual facial features and slipped covertly past the concierge at reception. The rogue reporter had no intentions of settling the cost of his overnight accommodation and crept quietly through the swivel doors that fronted the 5 star rated hotel.

The Sandmouth sea view was magnificent and the lanky felon looked over to his left to observe the sail-like netting that covered the neighbouring Living

Coast Zoo complex. Troon sniggered to himself and stiffened his coat-collar, as he made his way to the main road that led to the harbour. Black feathers began to appear from his coat-cuffs and his bended knees twisted inside his trousers to reverse his crooked stance, as he muttered under his breath. "That feels much better," he sighed and made a hasty dash along the pavement, as a multitude of lengthy tail-feathers emerged from the base of his coat. He shrugged his shoulders to discard the bulky clothing, as a pair of black wings spanned outwards.

Finally the villain pulled the trilby hat from his head to reveal the face of a coastal swimming-bird. He sniggered to himself again. "I can't believe those stupid policemen didn't work out that my name *Marc Troon* was an anagram of *Cormorant*... ha-ha – what idiots, some detectives they've turned out to be!" The Gullfather's messenger had used his disguise to great affect and now his true identity could be revealed, as he took to the air with his neck kinked in flight and then dived head first into the sea.

The Cormorant's angular profile entered the crashing waves like an arrow, as he sped beneath the surface and opened his hook-tipped bill to catch an unsuspecting mackerel. The large bird reappeared from the water and soared into the air to dry his feathers, as the blood from the struggling fish reddened the yellow patch at the base of his beak. Troon jerked his neck backwards and swallowed the fish whole, as he crooked his white throat to view the harbour below. The strong bird powered his flight and headed towards the clock tower, as he cried out with a deep harsh call. "Well that was absolutely delicious and a fine way to end my brief but interesting visit to this pathetic world of humans... my task is complete and the Gullfather will be pleased with my results – now, I'd better get back to the clock tower!"

Back inside the coastal zoo laboratory, D.I. Sharp and Detective Gribbon cowered to avoid the frantic activity above their heads. The room was now filled with a flock of disorientated pigeons and the two police officers covered their ears to douse the deafening sound of flapping wings.

Detective Gribbon managed to catch the eye of the delighted sorceress and repeated his previous question. "Where is Sereny Ugbrooke?"

Before the Flaglan could answer, the sound of another female voice echoed amongst the cooing pigeons. "I'm here!" announced the pretty blonde girl, as she walked calmly into view through the doorway. "Sorry to have messed you around, officers... but it was important to buy enough time to complete the first phase of the campaign before you eventually found me."

"It's great to see you are safe, Sereny... your mother is very worried about you!" said Detective Gribbon, as the pigeons flew higher and began to settle on top of the chain-suspended light fittings.

Sereny smiled, as the birds continued to coo in a choir-like manner above. "Thank you and don't worry about my Mum... I called her a few minutes ago – she's furious with me but at least she knows I'm okay."

D.I. Sharp interrupted. "But what is this campaign you both keep talking about?"

The young girl afforded Flaglan the wink of an eye, as she looked up and then turned to point at another flock of pigeons still waiting inside the aviary. Sereny repeated the comment made by the High Priestess. "As Flaglan said… this is your new police force and we need you to guide them to a very strange world far-far away in another time dimension – a place that we are all about to visit."

The two police officers struggled to comprehend the bizarre information being fed to them and Detective Gribbon asked. "So where are we supposed to be going then… Pathylon?"

Flaglan interjected. "No, not Pathylon… we're going to New York – but not the New York you know about!" she exclaimed. "It's a New York where feathered creatures reside… a New York that is in terrible danger!" She confirmed and picked up a small cutting device from the table, as she nodded to Sereny. "Ahhh… this will prove useful!"

"What do you need it for?" asked Sereny.

"You'll see!" laughed the High Priestess. "Now, we need to make our way to the clock tower… before the time portal that leads to the ancient path closes – we have to join forces with Bradley Baker and his friend Musgrove Chilcott!"

The two detectives did not get the opportunity to ask any more questions, as a cloud of blue swirling smoke filled the room and all the remaining pigeons flew into the laboratory. The room seemed to increase in size dramatically and more flapping wings appeared from the aviary to fill the space, as the police officers began to change form.

Sereny and Flaglan also started to transform into bird-like creatures, as the intensity of the smoke span into a tornado shape that collected every living creature in its path. The force of the spinning vortex lifted them upwards through the roof of the complex and out into the sunlit sky above the zoo.

Flaglan spread her short grey wings and glided through the air using her long tail to guide her, as she completed her transformation. The female Sparrow Hawk darted parallel to the edge of the netted-aviary and held out the cutting tool, as the wire-mesh separated to form a gaping hole in the enclosure. She squawked a cry of satisfaction as the rare sea-birds seized their opportunity to free themselves from their oppressive existence. One by one they escaped, as Flaglan's white undercarriage turned to compliment her transfixing personality.

Sereny followed the flighty antics of the newly formed High Priestess by taking on the bird-like features of a Sand Martin. Although her plumage was rather drab looking, her dark underwings contrasted with her white belly feathers and the brown band of quills around her breast tinged to compliment a shade of ochre-grey.

The transformed police officers were enjoying their new-found ability to fly and the two pigeons batted their banded wings profusely. The detectives fluffed out their glossy green and violet chests to lead the chasing flock of a thousand-or-so fellow pigeons, as their fast-beating underwings caught up with the leading female birds.

The Gullfather of New York

10

Weird Transformations

The activity above the coastal zoo continued with the swirling undercurrent of smoke keeping the group of feathered creatures together to form a magnificent display of flying prowess. Flaglan led the flock in an arrow-shaped formation towards the clock tower where Bradley and Musgrove were standing.

The frustrated boys had decided to check out the base of the monument again for more clues and were just about to finally close the door when a rapid shot of black feathers swept passed. "What was that?" asked Musgrove, as the speedy Cormorant disappeared inside the base of the clock tower.

Bradley rubbed his eyes in disbelief and exclaimed. "I could a sworn that was one of those horrible black seabirds… you know, the one's that my Dad complains about when we go fishing off the pier – they always try to pinch the mackerel off your line!"

"Do you mean a Cormorant?" replied Musgrove.

"Yeah… that's what the cheeky beggars are called – quick, let's shut the door before it escapes!" shouted Bradley.

The Sparrow Hawk responded to Troon's unwelcome entry into the clock tower and the High Priestess pushed her wings back to begin an aggressive nose-dive. She called down with an abundant staccato of shrieking sounds. "Ki'ki'ki'kik… stop – don't shut the door!"

Bradley was alerted by the ear-piercing cries from the Sparrow Hawk and he looked up, as the sunlight blinded his vision. Then Sereny released a distinctive rasping noise. "Ree'ree'reep'eep… Bradley!" she called to draw the attention to her presence. "It's me, Sereny… up here – you must leave the door open!"

The boy placed a saluted hand over his brow to shield the glaring sun from his eyes, as the Sand Martin flew past and kissed his head before disappearing through the narrow gap in the door. "Sereny... that was you!" gasped Bradley, as the Sparrow Hawk also swept passed and was quickly followed by a continuous line of pigeons led by the two winged policemen.

Musgrove looked on in disbelief, as the flock of birds shot past his head one-by-one. The pigeons filed through the doorway like bullets being fired from an automatic machine gun and the stunned teenager cried. "Where are they all coming from, Brad... and did you see the first two pigeons that went through - I swear one of them was my Uncle and the other was Detective Gribbon?"

Bradley waited for the last bird to enter the base of the clock tower and then pulled the door fully open. He jumped inside and encouraged his astonished friend to follow, as the oak-panelled door slammed shut behind them. "Sereny must have been behind another door... I guess my instincts were wrong but

I'm glad we stuck around to find out!" admitted Bradley. "At least our golden girl has been released and thank god she's alive!" He exclaimed, as a few wisps of light crept in through the clock tower window. The gentle rays of sunlight provided a dim glow to the small room and it supplied enough luminosity for the two boys to witness each other's imminent transformation.

Musgrove could feel his face starting to change shape and he rubbed his fingers over what felt like a beak growing in place of his nose, as he stated the obvious. "Whatever happened to Sereny and my Uncle is about to happen to us... it looks like we're turning into birds too!" He exclaimed and watched in amazement, as the eternal chosen one began to take on the form of an exotic looking *Jay*.

Bradley's checked shirt was replaced by familiar light-blue markings that appeared on the shoulders of his broad wings. Long black tail feathers developed with conspicuous white plumage around his rump and his grey wing tips spread outwards. The wingspan of the Jay filled the tiny space, as his chest became dusky pink and the feathers darkened to brown over his back to match what used to be his human hair. "Shreeek'shree-shreeek… this is unbelievable" cried Bradley with a loud harsh screech. "I've got wings!"

"Anyone would think we've been overdosing on those famous energy drinks… what a load of *red-bull*!" joked Musgrove. "Never mind your wings… take a look at me – I definitely wasn't wrong about the *red* part!" he shouted, as he pointed his wing tips at the bright plumage covering his chest and face. "I don't believe it… how come I get to be a *Robin* – we'll probably bump into *Batman* and *Catwoman* next!"

Bradley laughed a screechy reply. "You're so funny, Muzzy… I guess anything's possible – just hope the *Penguin* and *Joker* don't turn up as well!"

Musgrove chirped his retort. "With all this feathery stuff happening… the *Penguin* is definitely a possibility!" He sniggered and completed the inspection of his light-coloured underbelly. The agile Robin then twisted his neck to prod his short bill into the brown plumage across his upper wingspan.

"When you've finished grooming yourself... we'll see what happens next – in the meantime I'm going to try and get a message to Jefferson," said Bradley, as he bent down to locate his mobile phone. "He'll be wondering what the hell is going on," he assumed, as the ground produced a short tremor. "I think the next stage of our journey is about to start, Muzzy... thankfully I can still use the tips of my wings like fingers – so I'll give Jefferson a call before this floor gives way!"

The eternal chosen one managed to manipulate his wing tips to make the phone call and his American friend answered straight away. Bradley insisted that Jefferson go into the nearest bathroom and lock the door. "Has the coin started to vibrate since I last called you?"

"Yes... it's been shaking for few minutes and it's getting rather warm!" replied Jefferson.

"Good... if it gets too hot – put your phone on hands-free and hold the mobile flat so you can place the grobite on the screen!" insisted Bradley, as the sound of rumbling emanated from the floor beneath his feet again. "We have to hurry… stay on the line so we can maintain a connection between me and the coin – now, carry it carefully into the bathroom and place your phone on the side of the bath!" he ordered.

"Why?" queried Jefferson.

"Just do what I say… we've no time to discuss it – we need to get you to other side with the coin!" explained Bradley, as Jefferson sighed and followed his friend's demands. "Oh… and Jefferson?"

"Yes, Bradley?" replied the anxious boy.

"Get prepared for the journey of your life!" warned Bradley. "And get ready for a weird transformation!"

"What sort of transformation?" asked the puzzled boy.

The ground beneath the clock tower shuddered violently for the third time, as Musgrove laughed and shouted over Bradley's shoulder. "There's a pretty good chance that you'll change into a bird, mate… and I can't wait to see which one you become – just make sure it's not a *penguin*!"

Bradley frowned at Musgrove and he listened intently to the sound of Jefferson locking the bathroom door. The phone's hands-free setting continued to connect him to the coin, as the nervous boy climbed into the bath and placed his mobile phone carefully on the side of the tub. The grobite began to spin and it rose into the air before crashing down into the bath.

Jefferson decided to aid his journey by running water from the taps, as the coin rolled slowly towards the plughole. The room filled with a green mist and the grobite secured its position, as the centre of the coin began to open. The American boy's task was almost complete and he started to shrink, as the water lapped up around his face. He screamed, as the pull of the raging torrent sucked him through the hole in the coin. He held on frantically to the smooth round edges of the grobite and successfully kicked the metal grid free from the drainage outlet. The exhausted boy wriggled around until his weight combined with the coin and they finally dropped into the fowl-smelling water inside the U-bend.

Jefferson climbed onto the grobite, which acted as a temporary raft and at last the flow of clean water forced him around the bend in the pipe. He continued to cling to the coin and they were washed down the long drainpipe into the dark abyss.

Bradley heard the commotion through the handset, as the phone signal died and he simulated a thumbs-up signal to Musgrove with his wing tips. "He's done it... our American friend is on is way – hopefully we'll meet him on the other side pretty soon!"

"Let's hope so!" chirped the Robin.

At that moment the floor finally crumbled and gave way, as the two startled birds plummeted into the darkness. They instinctively spread their wings to steady their decent into the swirling vortex, as Bradley revealed. "And like the message on the coin stated... this must be the time portal that will take us along the ancient path and will hopefully lead us to the *Gullfather of New York*!"

11

A Second Clock Tower

Unbeknown to Bradley and Musgrove, a strange figure had been hiding inside the clock's winding mechanism in the apex of tower. The Magpie looked down from his lofty position to witness the broken ground reconstructing itself, as the rumbling noise continued. The disturbance did not prevent the three minute hands from moving simultaneously to the next digits, as the mischievous bird shuffled between the turning cogs.

The Gullfather's henchman passed through safely and reached out his clawed leg to feel the top rung of a wall-mounted ladder. He then began his careful descend until he reached halfway down the thin iron steps and waited for a few moments. The floor continued to reseal itself and the Magpie thought back to Bradley Baker's last telephone conversation with the American boy before he and the Robin plummeted into the abyss.

The intelligent and adaptable bird-creature was pleased to have witnessed the eternal chosen one successfully enter the time portal, as he rattled. "Cha'cha'cha'cha… challenge completed and the boy fell through my trap – it worked like a dream!" He boasted, as the metal ladder vibrated. The clock tower began the final stages of its transformation back into a solid monument and the confident bird squawked a harsh triumphant cry. "Placing the ribbon and the riddle near the door had the desired effect… at last, Bradley Baker is on his way to the great alternate Metropolis – now the Gullfather will be able to complete his giant masterpiece once the American boy has delivered the coin from the other side of the portal."

The ground was almost solid and the centre of the floor was about to close, as the particles of stone dust swirled downward into the abyss to create an inverted tornado. The distinct black and white feathers on the huge bird fluttered, as he jumped down to land safely at the edge of the shrinking hole.

The Magpie paused again and frowned. He knew he had made a fatal error, whilst tricking the boy hero into the time portal. Leaving one of his black tail feathers where it could be discovered near the clock tower had proved costly, as the troubled bird cackled to himself. "The Gullfather will not be pleased to welcome a sorceress Sparrow Hawk from Pathylon and thousands of pigeon police reinforcements... hopefully he will afford me some leniency – the capture of the eternal chosen one should make up for my small mistake." He then stared into the vortex and launched himself into the air, as he pulled back his wings in a dart-shape fashion. The bird's remaining tail feathers just cleared the eye of the sandstorm, as the last few particles of dust sealed the base of the monument. The Magpie let out a final squawk of regret. "No doubt that blue-eyed Cormorant will receive all the plaudits... I'd better get back before Troon takes all the glory!"

The turbulence created by the closure of the portal swept through the vortex and the resulting surge of air passed over Bradley Baker like a giant's breath. The boy hero was some hundred metres ahead along the spiraling corridor of time and was experiencing another rollercoaster ride. His newly-formed streamline body carried him at high speed like a bullet being shot through a gun barrel. Musgrove's *robin-wings* flapped frantically, as he struggled to keep up with his friend and flew a few metres behind the confident Jay. The two boys continued their fast pace and made good progress, as they closed in fast on the dense mass of pigeons flying ahead.

At the front of the flock, the underbelly of Sereny's *Sand Martin* plumage reflected in the tunnel's opaque translucency as she accelerated within the slip stream of the leading Sparrow Hawk. Flaglan opened her hooked beak and released another ear-piercing staccato, as she shrieked. "Ki'ki'ki'kik'ki'ke… keep up, golden girl – the second clock tower is not that far away!" she cried. "It won't be long before we reach the next portal… the exit from the vortex is located below the *Jersey Journal Building* and the *Kingfisher* will be waiting for us!"

Sereny sounded her reply and questioned the High Priestess. "Ree'ree'reep'eep… who is the *Kingfisher*?"

The Sparrow Hawk turned her head and cast a brow-curving look at the young Sand Martin, as she pulled her wings back to increase her speed. "*The Kingfisher* is the *Mayor* of New York… he governs Manhattan – we must help him to defeat the Gullfather and stop the evil gangster's acts of terrorism against the Metropolis!"

"Why are you involved… what's this got to do with King Luccese and Pathylon?" asked Sereny, as she too pitched her wings back and increased her speed to keep up with the powerful sorceress.

"If the Gullfather finishes his latest project and completes the secret weapon he is planning to build…

he will not only gain control and destroy all links to the island of Manhattan – but he will also have the power he needs to fire his weapon beyond New York!" replied Flaglan. "That means the whole world, parallel to yours… including Pathylon – would be in danger!"

Musgrove's uncle flew level with the exhausted Sand Martin to join the conversation. The senior New York pigeon policeman had overheard the reason for helping the Kingfisher to defeat the Gullfather and the newly promoted Captain Sharp of the N.Y.P.P.D. voiced his question. "What is this weapon you speak of, Flaglan?"

The Sparrow Hawk shook her crested head. "That is not known yet… it's a closely guarded secret - however, we do know that the *Gifted and Talented* children kidnapped by the Magpie will play an important part in its construction!"

The police officer beat his short wings profusely and puffed out his chest feathers, as he questioned how a small group of children could pose such a threat. "The Magpie stole just eleven children in Devon... don't you think you are overreacting a bit?"

Flaglan twittered in a shriek of laughter and turned her head to face the front, as the exit of the time portal appeared in the distance. "I'll let the Kingfisher explain the finer details... now, get ready everyone - we're about to enter the base of the second clock tower!" she revealed, as Bradley and Musgrove flew passed the trailing pigeons to join the leading birds.

Sereny's eyes shone brightly with an affectionate sparkle, as the eternal chosen one glided parallel to her wingspan. "Hello, Bradley... good to see you again – and I like your choice of bird!"

"Hi Sereny... not my choice, I'm afraid – but I guess a Jay is good enough!" he replied and tipped his wing to reveal Musgrove. "Take a look at *Robin* over there!"

"Well your colours certainly do suit you, Bradley... I especially like those blue feathers – they match your favourite shirt!" complimented the Sand Martin, as she chuckled at the sight of Musgrove. Sereny winked at Bradley and commented, as their

Sandmouth friend flew alongside them. "And you're plumage is looking rather resplendent and very bright... I'm liking the red – so where's *Batman,* Muzzy?"

The crested teenager scowled at the swallow-like bird and swooped to nudge Bradley playfully into the soft wall of the vortex. "Did you put her up to that... what have you been saying to Sereny?"

Bradley recovered from his friend's gentle push and ruffled his blue shoulder feathers back into shape, as he returned the wink of an eye to Sereny. "I think you're going to have to get used to the super hero inferences, Muzzy... but don't let it bother you – seriously, mate you look fab!"

Musgrove glared at the cheeky Sand Martin and then his eyes widened at the sight of the swirling exit a few metres ahead. Flaglan ignored the commotion behind her and continued to lead the flock, as she flung back her wings to slow her pace. The remarkable Sparrow Hawk cast her strong legs affront, as her sharp talons pierced through the exit of the vortex.

The Gullfather
of New York

12

The Gullfather's Elite

Above the portal entrance, the clock face on the *Jersey Journal* building still bore the scars from shrapnel created by the Black Tom explosion many years ago. The clock tower stood proud as a symbol of defiance against evil deeds and its red-brick exterior was a familiar sight on one corner of Journal Square in New Jersey.

A group of river-birds with cameras congregated around a trap door that led into the basement of the clock tower. The Kingfisher pushed his way through the crowd of journalist Oystercatchers inside the Jersey Journal building. A squadron of armed pigeon police stayed close to the Mayor. They wore the familiar New York blue uniforms with the letters *N.Y.P.P.D.* emblazoned on their gold cap badges, as they protected the government representative from any surprise attacks.

The New Jersey suburb was mob territory; as was the nearby Liberty Island, which had been claimed by the Gullfather since the damage caused during the Black Tom explosion. Back then, the Mafia boss had offered to pay for all the repairs to the broken statue and promised to reopen its torch and crown to the New York public. But the gesture of goodwill never materialized and the Statue of Liberty remained in his evil grip. No-one had since dared to cross the narrow stretch of water that formed part of the Hudson River or even board the ferry to Liberty Island.

The trap door flung open and the Sparrow Hawk climbed the wooden steps that led from the cellar below. The Kingfisher stepped forward to welcome Flaglan, as Bradley and Sereny appeared closely followed by Musgrove. "I'm so glad you have arrived here safely... welcome to New York – are the others with you?"

Flaglan's hooked beak curved upwards, as she smiled and her spotted plumage quilled. "You had better take a few steps backward, dear Mayor and open the main doors... there's a large flock of pigeons following me out of the time portal!" she exclaimed. "They will fill this room in seconds... I would advise you open those doors pretty quick!"

The Kingfisher heeded the Sparrow Hawk's advice and ordered his officers to open the large wooden doors, as the loud eerie humming sound of flapping wings echoed from the dark opening in the floor.

Bradley recognised the imminent danger and instinctively reached out to guide Sereny towards the safety of his chest. Musgrove copied his friend's actions and they all raised their feathered limbs to shield their faces, as the disoriented pigeons escaped from the vortex. The noisy flutter of fast-beating wings filled the basement room beneath the tower and the cooing birds headed straight for the sunlight, as the New Jersey skyline filled with a swirling grey cloud of newly recruited police officers.

The Kingfisher stepped forward and informed the new arrivals that a Cormorant had just escaped their futile attempts to capture him. "He was in a bit of a hurry... I guess he needed to report back to the Gullfather!"

Captain Sharp approached the Kingfisher and produced a note book. The word *CORMORANT* was written in capital letters and had been rearranged. "Is this the one you speak of?" he asked.

The Mayor of New York nodded. "Yes... your detective prowess will prove very useful here – it was indeed MARC TROON!"

Officer Gribbon stepped forward. "How did you work that one out, Sir?"

"I've had my suspicions for a while but I left it too late to act... that meddlesome reporter has eluded us – I just wish I'd followed up on my gut feeling!"

Musgrove sympathised. "It's not your fault, Uncle... none of us really knew what was going on – he played us all with that newspaper report!"

Bradley revealed his thoughts on the subject. "Musgrove's right… Troon's mission – or should I say the Cormorant's mission to get the local newspaper to print the story as a headline did enough to make us follow the trail of blue ribbons *and* the feather!"

Sereny intervened. "Yeah… and the Magpie sure played his part too!"

Bradley nodded and enquired. "And speaking of which… where is the so-called *Magpie* – did he pass through here Mr. Mayor?"

The Kingfisher shook his long bill, as Flaglan twitched her head and walked across the room towards the exit of the vortex. The Sparrow Hawk leaned down and held out her wing to summon the others. "Come over here and listen… I think I can hear something inside the time portal."

The Mayor obliged and stood next to the sorceress, as Bradley moved closer flanked by Musgrove and Sereny. The two pigeon police officers stood back, as the group of Oystercatchers readied their camera's to snap any impending action.

"I think our black and white friend is about to join us!" exclaimed Flaglan, as the noise from inside the vortex increased and everyone linked wings in readiness for the henchman's arrival.

As predicted, the time-travelling thief sped upwards out of the hole in the floor. "Cha-cha-cha-cha-cha!" rattled the Magpie, as he outstretched his magnificent white wing feathers and glided elegantly above the waiting crowd.

The pigeon police officers took to the air immediately followed by Bradley and Musgrove, as the flashbulbs from the Oystercatcher's cameras captured the fracas. The Magpie dipped and turned to elude his pursuers and headed for an open window. Flaglan pulled back her wings and intercepted the frustrated bird, as he diverted his flight path towards the main doors of the building.

"Stop him... Sorrow must not escape!" shouted the Kingfisher, as more pigeon police entered the clock tower.

"So that's his name!" screeched Bradley, as he flew down to help the Sparrow Hawk.

Musgrove followed the Jay and mirrored his friend's thoughts. "I wonder if he's married to another one called *Joy*?" he quipped and puffed out his red breast. "Who cares... it's time to take this *Sorrow* character down, Brad!"

"Too right, Muzzy... you take the left and I'll flank his right – that should give Flaglan and the pigeon police the opportunity to close in and grab him!" ordered Bradley, as he opened his wings and veered off.

Flaglan recognized the two boy's tactics and headed straight for the Magpie's tail feathers. She pulled her wings back and pushed out her talons, as they tore through Sorrow's long black tail feathers.

"Cha-cha-cha-cha!" rattled the Magpie, as his balance was thrown out of kilter. "You won't take me down that easily, Flaglan!" He cawed, as the two pigeon police officers grabbed his wings to render the Magpie helpless.

Bradley and Musgrove swooped to assist the assailants capture when a rush of wind blew into the clock tower from an open window, as a familiar black

134

sea-bird smashed into Flaglan's midriff with his hook-billed beak. The Sparrow Hawk reeled backwards and released Sorrow's tail feathers, as she was sent crashing into the tower wall. The resulting impact knocked her senseless, as she slumped down the side of the wall and hit the floor hard.

Troon had returned to help his troubled accomplice and the Cormorant was accompanied by a flock of two hundred-or-so rooks and ravens. The Jersey Journal clock tower was cram-packed with the Gullfather's elite henchmen and they quickly over-powered the uniformed pigeons, as the Kingfisher looked on helplessly.

Sereny screamed. "Watch out, Bradley!"

It was too late. One of the large muscular rooks dropped its beak and head-butted the frightened Jay into a girder supporting the roof. Bradley was knocked unconscious and a waft of distinctive blue feathers dislodged from his limp wings, as he was sent spiraling out of control into the vortex below.

"Ree-ree'ree-reep'eep... Bradley - nooooooooooo!" rasped Sereny again, as she flew down in pursuit of the eternal chosen one.

The harrowing cries of the Sand Martin disappeared into the abyss and the battle above ensued. The Magpie was released from Musgrove's desperate hold by the vastly superior ravens, as the aggressive crows flocked to aid their black-feathered allies. They successfully removed Sorrow from the building, as the Cormorant held out one of its broad wings and pinned the weakened Robin to the wall. "You mess with the Magpie... then you mess with me – you mess with me, then you mess with the Gullfather, you pathetic red-breasted human!"

Musgrove was struggling to breath and Troon released his strong grip, as the Robin slumped to the floor to join Flaglan. The pigeon police were decimated by the stronger birds and the two officers nursed their injured wings, as the Cormorant came face-to-face with the Kingfisher. "Let this be a lesson, dear Mayor... your pathetic attempt to get help from the outside world has proved futile – just as Don

Brando Ceeguloni predicted." He squawked. "However, the return of Bradley Baker was a good move and I must thank you for the part you have played in securing his arrival... however, his untimely death down that dark hole is a blessing – it has saved him from a torturous experience at the hands of the Gullfather!" Laughed Troon. "Now, all we need to do is find the coin and I'm sure the Crabtree boy will oblige us with that sacred gift... when we eventually find him!"

The Kingfisher trembled and issued a petrified response. "You may have won this battle, Troon... but the Gullfather will not succeed – the citizens of New York will fight to the death to stop that meddling gull getting his evil hands on our great metropolis!"

"Silence Kingfisher... you talk rubbish and I'm getting bored now!" replied the Cormorant, as he called to the remaining rooks and ravens inside the clock tower. "Come on, my friends... let us return to the Gullfather and inform the Don of our victory and the untimely death of the famous *Bradley Baker*!"

of New York

13

Return of the Shade Runner

A dense smog filled the polluted air and the evening closed in on the streets of New York in a remote part of the *Queens* district. One of the Gullfather's secret bases was situated along a poorly-lit back street in Long Island City and the rundown chemical factory took on the appearance of a disused warehouse. The dirty-looking façade of the industrial building boasted a sign board that masqueraded the unit as a storage facility, which held a dangerous secret within its broken-glass frontage.

Inside the dilapidated building, two creepy-looking figures crossed an elevated metal gantry that spanned the factory floor. Don Brando Ceeguloni was assisting a blind hooded character, who walked slowly with the aid of a special stick adorned with a silver skull. They had just arrived at the plant and a small team of speckled birds gathered round, as they began to converse with the Gullfather.

The starlings were revered in the area for their allegiance to the Mafia boss and their expertise in the mixing of chemicals. The flock of scientists were developing a toxic cocktail that would be guaranteed to help wreak havoc over the city and they had worked through the night to fulfill the latest order.

The Gullfather held a gasmask over his large yellow beak, as he clanked along the metal gridding. He looked down cautiously at several cylindrical vessels containing bubbling green waste and sniggered behind his protective disguise, as the dark figure continued to walk *wing-in-wing* by his side.

The sinister birds squawked a plotting conversation, as they approached an office at the far side of the gantry. The stranger was led towards a sliver of light that escaped through the doorway, as Don Brando

Ceeguloni ushered his partner-in-crime into the cigar-smoke filled room. They both entered and joined a congregation of intimidating gangsters, who were already seated around a large table.

A noxious smell of lethal fumes filled the air, as the mob leader pulled back a chair to allow the scraggy looking crow to take a seat, as the bird removed his brimmed hat to reveal a pair of darkened glasses that concealed his empty eye sockets. The new gang recruit sat in silence, as the huge gull introduced him to the select gathering of henchmen. "This fine fellow will be joining our quest to take control of Manhattan... the *Hooded Crow* has just escaped from a world we know as Pathylon and he has agreed to help us capture the eternal chosen one and of course secure the sacred coin!"

A sharp-suited raven called *Raith* addressed the Gullfather in a cautious manner, as he croaked. "How can we trust him... what does this *blind* weak bird have to offer us?"

The Don remained standing and afforded his black feathered associate a disapproving stare. "Raith...

you disappoint me – you dare to question my decision to recruit this reputed individual!" he squawked and smashed his clenched wing tip on the table. "I don't think you realize who this is... do you?"

"I'm sorry boss... I didn't mean to question your integrity – I errrr, wasn't thinking straight – please forgive me!" replied Raith, as he cowered back into his chair.

"That's always been your problem... you *don't* think – try engaging your empty brain before opening your beak!" scolded the Gullfather, as he offered an open wing to the stranger.

The Hooded Crow lent forward and outstretched his greyish-black wings on the table top, as he cawed a chilling response to uncouth raven. "I am a powerful *Shade Runner* with a score to settle... I may have lost my sight but I still possess the ability to defeat and capture my arch-nemesis, Bradley Baker!"

"A Shade Runner?" questioned Raith. "The only Shade Runner to survive the reign of King Luccese in Pathylon was... Ethan Darrrrrke – no, surely not, you can't be him?"

141

The Hooded Crow began to rattle his retort. "Caw-caw-caw… you insolent fool – how dare you doubt my existence!"

Raith sat back in his seat to action his retreat and responded. "Then you are the renowned evil apprentice of the Shadow Druid!"

The Gullfather interjected. "Silence… your continuous squawking is beginning to annoy me – afford our guest the respect he deserves and let's get back to main reason why we are all gathered here!"

Ethan Darke produced a raw smile and pushed his chair back, as he stood to address the Mafia hierarchy. "Firstly, I would like to thank Don Brando Ceeguloni for inviting me to join your esteemed organization… my reason for being here has a dual purpose – not only to seek revenge on *Baker* for inflicting a life of darkness on me but also to help you attain the gold coin you seek, which I believe will power the greatest weapon of all time!"

Before the Hooded Crow could finish his address the door of the office swung open and Troon entered the room followed by a disheveled looking Magpie.

The Gullfather insisted upon hearing why his two most feared henchmen were not only late for the meeting but had rudely interrupted the proceedings. "How dare you disrespect my authority, Troon and explain to me... why is Sorrow injured?"

The Cormorant apologized for barging in without knocking and explained the reason for their delayed arrival at the chemical factory. "We ran into a bit of trouble at the Jersey Journal building earlier... the Kingfisher was waiting for Sorrow to exit the vortex inside the clock tower – the Magpie was ambushed by some pigeon police reinforcements from the outside world."

Don Brando Ceeguloni approached the Cormorant and placed one of his feathered fingers beneath the seabird's bill. "You were only supposed to entice the boy and his coin into the vortex... I did not make any allowances for others to follow him from the outside world!"

Sorrow moved forward and insisted that the Cormorant had saved his life inside the clock tower. Troon then turned to address the group of hoods and informed them that thousands of pigeon police had been drafted into their world by a sorceress called Flaglan.

The Gullfather reacted angrily, as he removed his wing away from Troon and took his seat at the head of the table. "This is disastrous... if Flaglan is here then that means that King Luccese and most likely Meltor from Pathylon are planning something – they obviously fear my plans to build the greatest weapon of all time!"

Troon requested to speak again. "Don Brando... we also bring you some good news – you will be pleased to know that I struck the boy with my head and killed the eternal chosen one!"

The Hooded Crow rose to his clawed feet and smashed his clenched wing onto the table. "What's that you say... Bradley Baker - dead?" He cawed. "Impossible... it would take more than a simple head-butt to kill the eternal chosen one!"

The Cormorant was taken aback by the unrecognizable guest. "Who are you and how dare you doubt me?"

Ethan Darke lifted his clenched fist of feathers and opened them to unleash a direct force that hit Troon in the breast and knocked him back against the door. "Do not question me... I can assure you - Bradley Baker is *not* dead!"

The room went deathly quiet, as the Hooded Crow sat down calmly and placed his hat back on his head. Even the Gullfather remained stunned and silently impressed by the power extolled from the new member of his gangster mob.

The Cormorant got to his feet and puffed out his upper body, as he attempted to justify his assertion that the boy hero had been killed. "The boy fell like a lead weight into the time portal... no one could have survived that fall!"

The Gullfather broke his silence. "Enough!" He laughed in a deep and gruff retort. "For the sake of moving on with this meeting... let us assume that particular box has not been ticked – if the Baker boy is dead so be it!"

"But boss... I definitely killed him!" insisted Troon.

"I said that's enough... the only thing I'm interested in is the coin – did you retrieve the sacred grobite?" asked the intimidating gull, as the Cormorant lowered his bill. "Well... answer me you idiot – did you acquire the coin or not?"

The Magpie moved forward and spoke in a calm tone. "Don Brando... I can vouch for the fact that Bradley Baker does not have the coin – I overheard a telephone call inside the clock tower at the far end of the time portal."

"Then where is it?" demanded the Gullfather.

"The Crabtree boy has it, Sir!" replied Sorrow.

"Who is this Crabtree individual you speak of?" asked the Great Black-Backed Gull.

"Jefferson Crabtree... he's from New York!" explained the trembling Magpie.

The Gullfather stood out of his seat again and exclaimed. "You mean the coin has been here in New York City all the time!"

"No Boss... not exactly – the boy lives on the outside world in another New York," replied Sorrow. "But apparently he is travelling here... the coin was

146

activated by Bradley Baker – he used his mobile phone to send the Jefferson boy down the plughole!"

"Stop… I've heard enough – take Troon and seek out this Crabtree individual!" demanded the Gullfather. "Find the coin then kill him and anyone else who gets in your way… now both of you go – leave us!"

The deflated Magpie and the Cormorant left the room knowing full well what they had to achieve. The gold coin had to be found and Don Brando Ceeguloni sat down to explain the rest of his plan to the other waiting mobsters.

Raith spoke again. "If you don't mind me asking… what are the starlings concocting inside those vats, Gullfather?"

"The very substance that will enable the weapon to move with great agility!" teased the Mafia Leader.

"Can you be more specific?" asked the Hooded Crow.

"Of course," replied the Gullfather and invited one of the starlings to explain.

The white-coated scientist stepped forward and informed the intrigued group that one of the containers held a mixture of sodium nitrate and distilled water. "The solution is just about to reach boiling point and we will allow it to cool before adding sulphuric acid from one of the other tanks… this will result in the production of nitric acid."

"Why are you making nitric acid?" demanded Raith, as the nervous starling looked over to his boss for permission to answer.

Don Brando Ceeguloni interrupted and called an abrupt end to the meeting. "That will be all gentlemen… too much has happened and we have wasted enough time talking – we will have to reconvene after the coin is found, then I will reveal why we need the nitric acid and how it will play an important part in my grand plan to control Manhattan!"

14

Close Encounter with Morgough

Bradley Baker was very much alive, as predicted by the Shade Runner. The shaken boy opened his eyes and sensed a cold dampness against the feathers on his back. He was laying on a hard surface and the moisture against his skin stemmed from a slight trickle of water flowing along the passageway.

The puzzled Jay looked up at the rounded roof of the hand-painted tunnel and then sat upright against the cold concrete. He spread out his wings and was quickly reminded that his human form had taken on a bird-like appearance. He tried to remember what had happened and why he was now stranded in what at first appeared to be an old disused sub-way.

The walls were covered in Graffiti and Bradley stared at the luminous painted lettering. One particular word intrigued him and he read it out loud without thinking. "Morgough… I wonder what that means!" He mumbled in a confused manner and rubbed his brow to feel a lump beneath the short feathers, as a slight flashback appeared in his mind. He saw the beak of a large black bird striking his face and then nothing, as he shook his head. The confused Jay pulled himself up off the floor and looked down at his clawed feet.

Bradley suddenly realized that he was standing on a length of rail track, which to his disbelief started to vibrate. The noise inside the tunnel heightened substantially and his attention was then caught by an increasing bright light travelling towards him at great speed. Suddenly, two green hands appeared and grabbed the petrified boy's shoulders, as he was pulled back violently into a safety hole. The train whizzed past and he turned to find out what had taken hold of him. A brick wall was all he saw then he felt a thud to the back of his neck and fell to the floor again.

Further down the tunnel, Sereny Ugbrooke walked carefully along the rail track. The Sand Martin called out her friend's name. "Bradley Baker… where are you – can you hear me Bradley?" She reeped. "Bradley Baker… it's Sereny!"

There was no reply and the girl continued through the dank subway until she reached a bend in the tunnel. Sereny thought she had seen something move up ahead, so she crouched and lay her wings outstretched on the railway sleepers. She waited a few seconds and then noticed a human-like figure on its hands and knees. It looked like it was searching for something so she lay low until it stood upright. Sereny muttered to herself. "My god… what is that?"

The creature turned quickly and looked in the girl's direction. It stared for a moment and then carried on scanning the surrounding track. Sereny was close enough to make out the strangers clothing, which were torn and ragged. The tatty overalls were covered in grease and the creature appeared to be holding an extremely large spanner in one of its hands. She decided to confront the strange being and lifted her wings back against her slender body. "Hey… you – who are you?"

The creature's head turned quickly and its gruesome yellow eyes peered at the Sand Martin. "You are either brave or stupid!" he shouted. "I am Morgough… a street artist – are you his friend?"

"Who are you talking about… what friend?" replied Sereny, as she approached the creature.

"His friend!" replied Morgough, as he pointed at Bradley lying very still in the manhole.

Sereny rushed over and the creature lifted the spanner. "Stay back or I'll hit you as well!" He shouted and drew back his arm in readiness to strike at the startled Sand Martin.

"Ree-ree-reep-eep, there's no need to be violent… please calm down – I mean you no harm," called Sereny and began to distract the creatures thoughts away from its violent stance. Morgough lowered his arm and held the spanner by his side, as the girl continued to hold a logical conversation. "Why are you here, Morgough… you said you are a street artist – would you like to tell me a little bit more about yourself?"

Morgough's demeanor changed dramatically, as he sensed the girl's kindness and rare interest in why he existed alone inside the gloomy subway. "No one has ever bothered to show me any sort of kindness before… you seem like a nice person – what is your name?"

"Ree-reep, I'm Sereny Ugbrooke… if you don't mind me asking – what are you looking for?" enquired the girl.

"My other spanner… I have two of them – I need two spanners you see," explained Morgough. "I like hitting things!"

Sereny's confidence was increasing and she could just make out the mutated facial features of the creature, as she moved a little closer. "Did you hit my friend with one of your spanners?"

"Yes sorry… but I didn't want the train to kill him – it's *my job* to kill things down here," explained

Morgough. "Will you help me to find my other spanner?"

"Errrrr… okay," hesitated Sereny. The last thing she wanted was a mad mutated street artist hitting her with one spanner let alone two. Then she noticed one of Bradley's legs move so the brave girl decided to keep the creature talking. "Tell me more about yourself, Morgough… how did you end up down here?"

Morgough was delighted that the friendly bird was intent on asking more questions and he decided to stop looking for the spanner. "As I said, I used to be a street artist… most of my stuff was graffiti art – I created a character for my *tag* and during the many years down here hiding from the bird folk I've now become my character!"

"That's interesting… how do you feed yourself?" enquired Sereny, as she noticed Bradley's other leg move. "I mean a healthy looking chap like you must eat well!"

Morgough looked down at the felled boy and held up his spanner again. "Well he's definitely on the

154

menu… and so are you!" raged the mutated being, as his demeanor changed in an instant and he rushed at the frightened girl.

"Ree-ree-reep-eep!" screeched Sereny, as Morgough swung the spanner. The girl fell backwards and held out her wings to cover her face as the spanner came crashing down.

THUD! THUD! THUD!

"Sereny are you okay?" asked a familiar voice.

The Sand Martin pulled her wings apart to witness the smiling Jay looking down at her. "Bradley… ree-ree-reep-eep – I thought you were never going to wake up!" she squealed. "I thought we were both gonna's there for a moment!"

Bradley threw the second blood-stained spanner on the floor. "Well he was never going to find that thing… I had it all the time – I was just waiting the right moment to whack him!"

"Well you certainly left it till the last moment that's for sure… anyhow, we're both safe now – let's get back up to the others!" she exclaimed. "They'll be worried about us… the battle with the Gullfather's

155

henchmen in the clock tower wasn't going well – I just hope everyone up there is okay!"

Bradley felt the side of his head where the creature's spanner had landed and rubbed yet another lump, as he put his wing around Sereny. "Not sure how many more hits I can take in one day... but thanks for saving my life just now!"

The Sand Martin reeped an affectionate reply. "My pleasure... and thanks for saving mine too!"

The two relieved friends flew down the tunnel and soon reappeared from the time portal inside the Jersey Journal clock tower. Musgrove was waiting with Flaglan and he called out to alert everyone. "Hey... here they are – thank goodness you're both safe!"

"Did you have any doubts?" laughed Bradley, as the others gathered around to hear about their close encounter with the mutated street artist.

Captain Sharp listened intently and applauded the two young birds for their bravery. He then stated the obvious and insisted they regroup to make the necessary plans to find the eleven missing school children.

The Kingfisher interjected to confirm a much serious situation, which put a completely different emphasis on the task at hand. "Captain Sharp... I have to inform you that the number of missing children is a lot higher than you think!"

The pigeon police officers looked very concerned and both held out their wings to receive two scrolls from the Mayor. The remaining Oystercatchers rallied round to take more pictures of the ongoing incident, as Captain Sharp unravelled his coiled roll of paper. The first names to appear on the list were those of the missing gifted and talented school children from Devon. The police officer brushed away a tear and read them out one by one;

"Louis Smylie Wild from Landscove, Emily Brown from Marldon, Ava Sutherland from Berry Pomeroy, Kyeesha Bryson from Harbertonford, Lucy Kies from Stoke Gabriel, Grace McLachlan from Broadhempston, Elliott Burrows from Dartington, Niamh Nolan from South Brent, Maisie-Eleanor Murray from Harbertonford, Charlotte Meakin from Marldon and Sereny Ugbrooke from Sandmouth!"

"Did you just say Sereny Ugbrooke?" asked Bradley.

"Yes… Sereny's name is definitely on the list!" replied the police officer.

Musgrove exclaimed. "But Sereny wasn't captured by the Magpie… so why is her name on the list?"

Captain Sharp shrugged his shoulders and looked over to Flaglan. "Do you have any idea why the young lady's name is on this list?" He asked. "And by the way there are hundreds more names on here!"

The Sparrow Hawk stepped forward and explained that she hid Sereny behind the door in her laboratory so that the Magpie wouldn't find her. "The door in the clue was always the one at the base of the clock tower."

Bradley punched the air in delight. "I knew I was right about that!"

Sereny spoke out to surmise why she had been included on the scroll. "I'm not surprised my name is on the list… the other pupil's names you mentioned, all took part in a writing competition hosted by a local children's author in Devon – I attended the workshops too so it definitely has something to do with *gifted and talented* school children!"

"Why do you say that brainbox?" teased Musgrove. "I've been recognised as a gifted and talented student at Sandmouth School as well!"

"Ree-ree-reep-eep... I didn't say you hadn't!" responded the Sand Martin in a sarcastic manner. "I'm on the list because it's obviously linked to pupils that attended similar courses - that's why, dumbbell!"

Bradley laughed at Sereny's witty retort and then asked the police officers to count the number of children on both lists. The two uniformed pigeons quickly summed up the total and Captain Sharp announced. "Six hundred and thirty five!"

The Kingfisher continued to deliver the results of the city's investigation into the Gullfather's activities so far. "We are assuming he has collected a child for every day of the year... hence the number 365 and who knows what he has done with them – we may be wrong but it seems the most logical answer," he explained. "And we have evidence that the head of

159

the mob has been spotted near an old chemical factory in Long Island City… we are also concerned that he still controls access to and from Liberty Island – and has done so for the past forty-or-so years since the Black Tom explosion, so the Statue of Liberty may hold the key to all this mayhem!"

Captain Sharp rolled up his scroll and handed it back to the Kingfisher. "Well at least we have something to go on and I'm confident we have a good team to solve these mysteries… I assume Mr. Mayor that you would like me to take over the investigation?"

"That would be most gracious of you, Captain Sharp… the populous of Manhattan will be served well – I'm sure," replied the Kingfisher, as the flashing of bulbs continued to illuminate the room, as the Oystercatchers took even more pictures.

Captain Sharp nodded in respect of the trust placed in him by the Mayor of New York and then raised his voice, as he pointed to the annoying photographers. "Can we get these snap-happy birds out of here, please?"

Bradley moved out of the way to allow the disgruntled Oystercatchers to be escorted out of the clock tower and then made a very important announcement. "Aren't we all forgetting something?"

Flaglan supported the eternal chosen one and anticipated the response. "The coin!"

The boy hero smiled and echoed the sorceress. "Yes... the coin – and the latest message it has revealed!"

Captain Sharp queried the importance of the sacred grobite. "What has the coin and its message got to do with anything?"

Flaglan answered the acting police chief in a clear and assertive tone. "Bradley is right about the importance of the coin... it is what the Gullfather enticed the *eternal chosen one* here for in the first place – Don Brando Ceeguloni needs it for whatever reason and I've got a feeling he won't care who he kills to get his grubby feathers on it!"

The Gullfather of New York

15

Forty Years in the Planning

Meanwhile on Liberty Island, an entourage of seagulls and ravens flew down and landed near the entrance to the magnificent monument. The dull laughing cries from the juvenile gulls echoed against the star-shaped walls of the building, as they pecked at scraps of food discarded by workers from the crown of the statue above.

The Gullfather had made a special journey to his headquarters beneath the Statue of Liberty following his meeting at the chemical factory. As he entered the base of the statue, the noise of high-pitched whistling could be heard deep underground in the purpose-built dungeons. The locked cells were crammed full of *gifted and talented* school children that had been stolen from the outside world. They were now transformed into penguin chicks and the whistling noise was the sound of their hunger. The choice of juvenile flightless birds for the children had been purposely planned to prevent them from escaping.

Don Brando Ceeguloni was accompanied by the Hooded Crow and Raith. They had been invited to oversee the final construction of the 365 purpose-built cages. "Ethan, my friend... I'm so pleased you decided to join me on Liberty Island – you'll be fascinated to see how my team of workers are making the finishing touches to the intricate body parts that will complete my new weapon of destruction!"

The Hooded Crow's thoughts were elsewhere and he could not stop thinking about the battle with Bradley Baker when the boy took his sight. Ethan Darke sniggered and cawed a grateful response, as he vented his thoughts out loud. "I'm confident that Bradley Baker is still alive and therefore I'm very keen to be part of your weapon building process, Don

Brando.... if the boy hero has survived the fall into the time portal - I would be most honoured to take the helm of your great weapon when it is completed!" He declared. "So I can destroy the eternal chosen one... once and for all - should he decide to challenge your control over Manhattan."

Raith rattled his approval, as he followed the Gullfather and Hooded Crow deep into the base of the great statue. The Mafia boss welcomed the Shade Runner's comments and sealed his allegiance to Ethan Darke by offering to reveal the purpose of the special cages. They continued down a series of stone staircases until they reached the dungeons that imprisoned the 364 penguin children.

Ethan Darke had developed a sixth sense that enabled him to see shapes through the evil glints inside his empty eye sockets. He could just make out the torn school uniforms that hung like threads from the malnourished chicks. The Shade Runner commented on the conditions in which they were being kept. "Are you not concerned that these children will starve or die of some disease?"

164

"That's no matter for your concern... soon their brains will be connected to their own light-weight cages – it's only their *gifted and talented* minds I'm interested in preserving!" squawked the Gullfather. "Once all 365 children are connected together... they will be as one – you'll find out soon enough my dear friend!"

The Hooded Crow questioned the ruthless mobster about the exact quantity of imprisoned penguins. "You say that all 365 children will be connected... according to the number count on the wall – you appear to be missing one child!"

"Well-spotted, my dear Ethan... you are right – your extra-sensory powers are working well," commended the Gullfather, as he pointed to a large notice board depicting the shape of the Statue above. He lifted his cane and rested the end on a girl's name written in the crown of Liberty. "This one keeps eluding us... but no worries – once the coin has been retrieved, the Magpie will seek out the golden girl and bring her here so we can place her in the brain of my lethal weapon!"

The Hooded Crow stared through his empty eye-sockets and concentrated on the list of names, as an image appeared in his mind. "Sereny Ugbrooke… that's Baker's girlfriend – how interesting!"

Raith interrupted the conversation and relayed a message to the Mafia boss, as a broad smile spread across the beak of Don Brando Ceeguloni. The Hooded Crow sensed a positive result and enquired as to the subject of Raven's news. The Gullfather rolled his feathered fingers and reached into the top pocket of his jacket to remove a fat cigar. He had been waiting for this moment for a long time and revealed his delight. "Forty years in the planning… and now I can complete my wonderful new toy – at last the coin is within my grasp!"

"I take it that Troon and Sorrow have found the Crabtree boy?" asked the Hooded Crow.

Raith could see that the Gullfather was too busy lighting his celebratory cigar and he nodded to acknowledge Ethan Darke's question. "Jefferson Crabtree has been sighted but not yet captured… the boy seems to have retained his human form so is proving a little too elusive – we have just dispatched more gulls and terns to assist in his capture."

Don Brando Ceeguloni finished lighting his cigar and placed the smoking tube of tobacco leaves in the corner of his large bill. "Where was the Crabtree boy spotted?" He asked and puffed heavily on the cigar.

Raith confirmed Jefferson's last known position. "At the entrance to the Empire State Building, Boss!"

"Ahhhh… how wonderful and how ironic he should be sighted near my intended target," replied the smug gull, as he invited Ethan Darke to follow him into a nearby storeroom.

The Hooded Crow was intrigued and he again questioned the Gullfather's comment. "What relevance does the Empire State Building have in relation to your planned weapon of destruction?"

"Patience, patience… my dear fellow," goaded the squawking gull, as he entered the huge storage facility that contained the metal cages. "As I said… all will be revealed very soon – now, let me show you the ingenious cradles that will hold those talented penguin miniatures for the rest of their pathetic little lives inside my beautiful new toy!"

Meanwhile back inside the Jersey Journal building, a very proud Captain Sharp had completed the assignment of each member of his new task force. Many squadrons of pigeon police officers had been dispatched all over the five boroughs of the city; from the Bronx to Brooklyn and Staten Island across Manhattan to Queens.

Lieutenant Gribbon called everyone to the centre of the room adjacent the entrance to the clock tower vortex. "The pigeon's will ensure law and order is maintained on the streets... now the Captain would like to make his final dispatches - please gather round to hear what he has to say!"

A circle of differing species of birds with concerned faces and multi-shaped beaks looked inward at the portly police chief. Once the group had settled and their inquisitive squawking had fallen silent, Captain Sharp proceeded to read out the names detailed on his notepad. "Mr. Mayor... I suggest you and your dignitaries make your way back to City Hall in Lower Manhattan – I can cover things from here!"

The Kingfisher nodded. "Very well Captain... I will leave the mission in your capable hands – I have no doubts that you and your friends from the outside world will capture the Gullfather and stop his evil plans to destroy our great city.

As the Mayor and his staff left the confines of the clock tower, Captain Sharp continued with instructing the assignments. "Lieutenant Gribbon... I'd like you to take Musgrove and Sereny with you to check out the chemical factory in Long Island City – we need to find out what poisonous cocktails the Gullfather is mixing in there!" He then turned to the Sparrow Hawk. "Flaglan... now you have recovered – I'd be grateful if you and Bradley could concentrate your efforts on finding Jefferson Crabtree and the coin!"

Bradley puffed out his plumage, as he stepped forward and fluttered his wings. "I must remind you all about the conversation between the seagulls in Sandmouth," he confirmed. "The Gargoyle specifically told us that the sacred grobite will act as

169

some kind key to trigger the Gullfather's secret weapon... but don't worry we'll find Jefferson and the coin – we must secure their safe return before the Mafia boss gets his feathery fingers on them!"

Captain Sharp saluted the bold statement from the eternal chosen one and insisted that everyone fly off to complete their assignments. A mumbling of voices ensued, as the room started to empty and Musgrove shouted. "What about the Gullfather?"

Before the police officer could reply, the shattering of glass cascaded down from an arched window above their heads and the loud flutter of huge black wings burst through the opening. An enormous white-hooded bird of prey landed in the centre of the room and the majestic creature cricked its neck from side-to-side. The bald eagle blinked its piercing eyes and shook its body to straighten the pristine feathers along its muscular frame, as it bellowed a stern reply. "Leave the Gullfather to us!"

Bradley looked at Flaglan's response and then noticed an unusual pair of short horns that adorned the huge bird's white crown of feathers. The Sparrow

Hawk seemed very pleased to see the great bird. She flew over and landed next to the eagle's sharp talons and congratulated his safe arrival. "Glad you managed to survive the arduous journey from Pathylon in time to help us, my lord... I'm pleased to hear the vortex inside the Met Life Building is still intact!"

As soon as Flaglan spoke the words *my lord*, Bradley recognised the bald eagle's friendly eyes and the Devonian horns now made perfect sense. "King Luccese... is that you?"

"Yes, young Bradley... it is good to see you and your friends from Sandmouth again – I wasn't expecting to call upon your services so soon after your last adventure, but it would appear the Gullfather's actions could also pose a threat to Pathylon!" replied Luccese.

Sereny flew down to join Bradley and at that moment the Eagle King was joined by five more majestic looking birds. The Sand Martin instantly recognised Ploom with her unusual six legs and she commented on the Klomus Hawk's appearance. "I see you have fully retained *your* bird-like form!"

"There was no reason for me to change!" replied Ploom. "My hawk-like prowess will be well-suited for this particular mission!"

The Sand Martin nodded and turned her attention to the unusual species of bird standing awkwardly next to Ploom. The exotic looking finch had orange-coloured feathers and Sereny screeched in delight. "Grog… is that you?"

The recently elected High Priest for Krogonia squawked a friendly retort from his parrot-like bill. "Kree'kree-kree, hello Sereny… you look, errrm – really good in your new feathered attire!" he joked and moved to wrap his dark-shaded wings around the fledgling Sand Martin. "I'm glad you recognised me through this stupid disguise… not sure if being a Parrot Crossbill is suited to the look of an intimidating Krogon Warrior– but I guess it will have to do!"

"Ree-ree-reep-eep, the colours really suit you, Grog… it's great to see you again - I've missed you so much!" cried Sereny and wrapped her tiny wings tightly around the powerful finch's rotund waste.

Guan-yin also made herself known to the astonished crowd of onlookers. The High Priest for the Blacklands had taken on the form of Green Woodpecker and she tilted her narrow beak to reveal a crown of bright red feathers. "Kle'kle'kle... it's great to see you all again!"

That just left two more members of the royal party to be formally introduced. A Kestrel and a Buzzard had also made the incredible journey from Pathylon via the time portal inside the Met Life Building on Madison Avenue. The two smaller birds of prey flew down and landed either side of the bald eagle, as the King of Pathylon held out his enormous wing span to afford a magnificent back drop. "Bradley Baker... I'm sure you will be pleased to meet two people very dear to you – Meltor and your Uncle Henley!"

Bradley look stunned. The Jay stepped forward to focus his glazed eyes on the two splendid birds of prey. Both Henley and Meltor moved away from the King's wingspan and held the boy, as Bradley uttered. "I never thought I would see either of you again… I'm overwhelmed – I feel so much better knowing you are here to help us."

Captain Sharp bowed, as the policeman offered his pigeon wing and shook the feathered fingers of the Bald Eagle. "Your majesty… the N.Y.P.P.D. is at your service!"

King Luccese insisted that the New York Pigeon Police Department continue to organize the campaign to remove the threat posed by the Gullfather and offered a supportive statement. "My High Priests and I have flown from Pathylon to help assist you in your mission… please carry on as you were – as I said when we arrived, leave the Gullfather to us!"

Henley afforded his nephew a rare smile and the boy reciprocated with a brief wave of his wing. "I'll catch up with you later, Bradley… be great to find out how your Mum and Dad are doing in the hotel business!" he shouted and then joined the others to discuss tactics with Captain Sharp and the King.

Flaglan squinted her sharp eyes and glared at Henley for mocking the eternal chosen one, as she spoke quietly to Ploom. "How long does he intend to keep up this pretense... he'll have to tell Bradley the truth eventually."

The Klomus Hawk insisted that the sorceress curb her tongue. "Please Flaglan... do not say anything to the boy – he will be devastated when he finds out his true identity!"

Flaglan fumed and turned away. "I just hope Henley is ready for the backlash... Bradley Baker is not going to take the news lightly!"

Ploom and the disgruntled Sparrow Hawk joined Meltor, who quickly excused himself. "Would you mind if I spoke alone with Bradley for a few moments?" requested the Galetian High Priest.

"You're not going to tell the boy about Henley are you?" pleaded Ploom.

"Of course not... that is something Bradley should never know – do you understand?" insisted Meltor and afforded Flaglan a stern glare, as the sorceress lowered her beak. The grey-spotted Kestrel moved away to approach Bradley and put his wing around the young Jay.

"Hi Meltor… it's great to see you again," enthused Bradley. "How's the heart… beating as strong as ever, I hope?"

Meltor smiled and acknowledged the boy's best wishes. He then proceeded to deliver some news that he felt the boy *had* to know, so Bradley could prepare himself for a certain unwelcome encounter with an old enemy. Luccese had not mentioned anything about the Shade Runner so the old Galetian whispered. "Ethan Darke has escaped from Pathylon and he is here in New York… the evil Shade Runner has been recruited by the Gullfather - I just thought you should know."

Bradley did not respond and instead contemplated the possible rematch with his sworn adversary. He uttered under his breath. "This adventure is turning out to be a bit of a nightmare… unexpected events certainly look like they are going to test my resolve this time round – Ethan Darke will be harbouring some pretty bad feelings about me, that's for sure."

16

Dead or Alive

Thousands of screeching seagulls and terns circled above the Empire State Building where Jefferson Crabtree was last sighted. A flock of ravens arrived in support led by the Magpie and followed close behind by Troon the Cormorant. The Gullfather's senior henchmen ordered the seagulls to land and search the side streets for the American boy.

The Magpie split from the group and took the ravens with him down to streetlight level, whilst Troon guided the terns to the top of the iconic skyscraper. Their objective was to recover the coin undamaged and ensure its safe delivery to the

Gullfather. However the fate of Jefferson Crabtree rested totally in the wings of his pursuers and an order was issued to take the boy *dead or alive*.

The search proved futile. Jefferson had taken to the sewers and he had reached a junction in the tunnel between 5th Avenue and West 34th Street. He could hear the frantic squawking of birds in the streets above, as his human form waded through the smelly water. "The power of the coin must be the only thing keeping me from changing into a bird… it's the only explanation I can think of," he muttered and headed straight down a tunnel parallel to East 34th Street.

Troon was becoming very frustrated at the lack of progress and the Cormorant ordered the terns to follow him down to the streets. "I've got an idea… to me, humans are like rats and I know where rats live – in the sewers!"

Jefferson was in immediate danger and he could hear the manhole covers above his head being ripped out of the road surface. The sound of busy traffic combined with the screeching of seagulls penetrated the sewers, as the Cormorant dived down with a dense flock of terns in a single line pursuit.

Meanwhile in Long Island City, Musgrove and Sereny had located the chemical factory with the help of Lieutenant Gribbon. The three novices had managed to climb in undetected through a broken window and made their way quietly past the security office. A narrow corridor led them to the main processing area but they were too late. The large vats of acid had been removed and all that remained inside the huge plant was a piece of paper that had been dropped on the floor.

Sereny reached down to retrieve the document. "It's a delivery note!" she exclaimed and read out the destination address. *"The Statue of Liberty, Liberty Island, New York... c/o the Gullfather!"*

"We had better get back and inform the others." Suggested Musgrove. "This place is deserted... there's nothing more for us to do here."

Lieutenant Gribbon took the delivery note and read the inventory details before folding the paper in half.

"The shipment contains 25 vats of Nitric Acid... that's a lot of dangerous liquid to be handling in one delivery – I've got a bad feeling about this!"

Back in Manhattan, Bradley and Flaglan had been tipped off about a commotion near the Empire State Building and they soon arrived at the scene. The pigeon police were fighting frantically with seagulls on every street corner, as the Cormorant continued his systematic search of the sewers below.

Jefferson was out of breath and was struggling to wade through the putrid waste. He stopped to rest for a while and sat back against a meshed grill, as the smell of excrement penetrated his nostrils. "Ergh, what's that?" he exclaimed, as a large white bird appeared on the other side of the grid. "Who are you?" the boy asked.

"I am the Great Ospera... I control an underground network of bird-spies – it's very rare that we see humans in New York, especially down here in the sewers!" stated the large Osprey. "You must be the one the Gullfather is looking for… that means you must have the sacred coin!"

"Do you work for the Gullfather?" asked Jefferson and stepped back nervously from the opening.

The Osprey ignored the human, as she effortlessly pulled the mesh away from the gap and the popping rivets ricocheted against the damp brickwork. The intimidating bird displayed her mottled white under-belly, as she stepped through the gap and confronted the helpless boy. "Do not be afraid… just give me the coin and I will let you go free!"

"I'll take that as a yes, then… you do work for the Gullfather!" exclaimed Jefferson, as the Osprey spread her impressive brown wings and released an ear-piercing cry.

"Of course… he pays me well and I am soon to become officiated into his elite flock of henchmen after the weapon is complete – now give me the coin or I will have to kill you!" threatened the bird of prey.

"Not so fast!" shouted the female Sparrow Hawk and smashed her head into the Osprey's midriff.

"Flaglan… what are you doing in New York?" shouted Jefferson, as another familiar looking bird arrived on the scene. "Bradley Baker… you took your time - thank god you've found me at last!"

"Hi Jeffers… glad you survived your first solo plughole experience!" replied the Jay and assisted the sorceress by drawing back his wings, as he kicked his agile legs against Ospera's face. Feathers scattered in all directions, as the huge bird crashed against the side of the tunnel.

Jefferson's attention was drawn to a loud noise of flapping wings and he tried to warn the Sparrow Hawk, as a flock of enemy reinforcements arrived on the scene. "Flaglan… watch out!" he cried, as Troon flew ahead of the terns. The Cormorant ignored the sorceress, as he pushed the startled boy to the floor and started to peck at his face.

Bradley saw what was happening to his friend and managed to fly clear of the fracas leaving Flaglan to fight the terns alone. The eternal chosen one struck a heavy blow to the Cormorant's head sending him reeling backwards, as Jefferson rolled over in agony.

Bradley jumped on Troon again and pushed the sea-bird's head beneath the water, as a spluttering of bubbles appeared on the surface. The black feathered henchman struggled to fend off the powerful Jay and his body fell limp, as the exhausted bird called over to his friend. "Are you okay, Jeffers?"

"Yes… it's just my face that hurts – that ugly thing has beaten me up pretty bad!" complained the boy. "But don't worry about me… go and help Flaglan – she's still in trouble!"

Bradley looked over to where the brave Sparrow Hawk was desperately fighting off a tirade of pecking beaks, as the terns continued their relentless attack. Then the sorceress took a nasty blow to her neck from the Osprey, as she fell back and hit her head against the sewer wall. Flaglan received another hard blow to her head and lay injured, as her eyes rolled. The Osprey started to laugh at the expense of the comatose hawk, as she held up the sacred grobite. "I think you've dropped something!" she screeched and looked over to Jefferson. "Better check your pockets, human… and get ready for a new look!"

"Is it true, Jeffers… has she got my coin?" asked Bradley, as he noticed some brown feathers beginning to appear on the boy's face.

"I'm afraid so, Brad… it must have fallen out of my pocket during the fighting!" replied Jefferson, as his human features began to transform into a bird-like creature. "I'm changing… oh no this feels weird, Brad – please help me!"

Bradley was powerless to aid Jefferson's plight and watched his friend complete an amazing transformation, as the dull light inside the sewer revealed an intricate mix of black, white, brown and grey plumage. Jefferson's cries for help became a rapid series of hoots. "Hoo-wooh… ho-ho-wo-woo-wooh!" he called, as the size of his eyes increased dramatically and he turned into a Tawny Owl.

The Great Ospera laughed at the boy's expense and gloated. "You and your friends have failed, Bradley Baker… I have the coin and the Gullfather will now be able to complete his masterpiece!" She squawked and her moment of glory was interrupted, as more mobsters arrived in the sewer.

The cawing ravens gathered around the Osprey and the Magpie pushed his way to the front of the squabbling crowd. Sorrow held out an open wing and demanded the coin be handed over. "I'll take that... thank you very much!"

"Not a chance!" replied Ospera. "I want to present the sacred grobite to Don Brando Ceeguloni in person – he promised me I'd become one of the elite!"

Sorrow released a sinister caw and placed his wing-tips against the Osprey's throat. "There's no place for putrid smelling sewer scum like you around the Gullfather's table... now hand over the coin before I squeeze the life out of you!"

Bradley whispered to Jefferson. "This situation is bad and losing the coin is disastrous... there's too many of them and we need to inform King Luccese – we got to get out of here," he muttered, as they edged away slowly against the curved walls and reached a ladder that led up to a manhole. "This is our chance to escape... you head up first and I'll keep a look out!"

The sound of the Osprey's dying groans could be heard in the distance and Bradley stepped on to the first few rungs of the ladder. He looked up to witness Jefferson lift the metal cover and started to ascend.

Then something caught his leg and the Jay turned in horror to see the Magpie's evil face staring up. "Going somewhere?" cawed Sorrow and took a firm grasp of Bradley's clawed foot and pulled down, as the Jay frantically held on to the ladder with his wingtips. "Not so fast Baker boy… you're going nowhere!"

Bradley made a last desperate attempt to evade capture, as he looked up and shouted to Jefferson. "Go… leave me – I'm done for!" he cried. "Just make sure Luccese and Meltor get to the Gullfather and stop him… before it's too late!"

Jefferson was left with no choice, as he witnessed the eternal chosen one being dragged into the sewer by the aggressive henchman. Tears welled up in the owl's large round eyes, as the sound of Bradley's ailing cries disappeared into the distance. The newly formed bird took to the air, as he flapped his wings at a fast pace and headed in the direction of Jersey City to deliver the bad news to King Luccese.

17

Left for Dead!

Under the dark of night, a convoy of delivery trucks arrived at the Liberty Island ferry crossing point in Lower Manhattan. The heavy goods vehicles were parked next to the jetty and the drivers dismounted from their cabs to await assistance, as a flock of crows and ravens appeared above the port. The Gullfather's crew of gangsters swooped down in a crude formation and a scraggy raven stepped forward.

Raith spoke briefly with the drivers and led the regimented off-loading of the heavy vats of acid from the factory. The pallets of toxic substance were fork-lifted onto the deck of a waiting ferry boat and the raven cawed loudly at the captain of the huge barge. "We'll meet you on the island!" he shouted and gathered the rest of the rattling entourage, as they took to the skies again.

Over on Liberty Island, the Gullfather waited patiently on the entrance steps at the base of the statue. The intimidating gull puffed on his cigar, as the Hooded Crow stood close by in readiness for the shipment of acid to arrive.

News about the capture of the coin had already been communicated and the Mafia boss was feeling very smug. A nervous starling appeared from the building and relayed another message to Don Brando Ceeguloni. "The construction is nearing completion, boss… the young penguins are just being fitted into their cages and the foreman has asked that you come down – he wants to make sure you are happy with the formation layout before we connect their brains to the main structure."

The Gullfather nodded and stretched out his magnificent black wingspan. "Very well… tell him

I'll be down immediately!" he confirmed, as the ferry sounded its eerie foghorn and approached the island's wooden pier. The mobster asked the Hooded Crow to stay. "Ethan... please make sure the delivery is off-loaded safely and stored inside the base of the statue – then get the starling technicians to connect the containers of nitric acid to the valves."

"What are you going to do with the acid?" asked the Hooded Crow in an inquisitive tone.

The Gullfather laughed. "All will be revealed within the hour... just make sure the lethal fluid is connected to the pipes - I don't want any mistakes at this late stage!"

The Shade Runner cackled a menacing reply. "Don't worry Don Brando... I'll ensure the task is carried out just as you ordered – I can't wait to see what you've been working on all these years!"

"The spectacle will be worth the wait!" cackled the gull, as he pointed his wing towards the arm of the statue. "You see the torch at the end of Liberty's arm?"

Ethan Darke crooked his neck and focussed his mind on the outline of the damaged limb, which was still covered in scaffolding. "Yes… I can just about visualize the cracks in the copper structure… what relevance does the torch have?"

The Gullfather walked to the top of the steps and opened the huge doors, as he offered the crow a final retort. "That torch, my friend will emit the greatest force ever created… once the arm is repaired and all the cages are in place!" He screeched. "Then all we need is the Ugbrooke girl and the coin… and speak of the devil - here's the Magpie now and he's holding the *sacred grobite*!"

Sorrow landed on the steps and handed over the coin to his delighted boss. "Hope I didn't keep you waiting too long, Don Brando!"

"No, no… your timing is perfect – how did you come across the coin?" asked the Gullfather, as he walked back down the steps to rejoin the Hooded Crow and called over to the waiting starling. "Tell the foreman I will be with him shortly… I just need to get an update from the triumphant Magpie!"

Sorrow proceeded to inform the mobster that the Great Ospera had refused to hand over the coin. "The stupid sewer spy was having some delusions of grandeur... she was rattling on about joining your elite henchmen, so I eradicated her - just as you ordered, Gullfather!" He then explained that Jefferson Crabtree had escaped and the eternal chosen one had been badly beaten. "We tortured him for hours but he wasn't prepared to tell us the whereabouts of the Sereny Ugbrooke... so we left for him for dead in the sewer with his Sparrow Hawk friend – the rats will most probably have eaten them by now!"

"Excellent work, Sorrow... so all that is left to do is locate the Ugbrooke girl!" squawked the Gullfather, as a familiar scraggy bird reappeared. "Ahhhh... and here is Raith – has the barge docked safely?"

"Yes Boss... they are just unloading the cargo now – it will be ready to transport into the statue in about ten minutes!" replied the Raven, as he flew back to the dockside.

The Gullfather squawked another confident retort. "Things do seem to be going swimmingly to plan... don't they, Ethan?"

Ethan Darke tipped his hat and made light of the situation and referred back to the Magpie's comment about Bradley Baker in the sewer, as he stared at Sorrow through his empty eye sockets. "Everyone keeps assuming the boy hero is dead... you are all fools to underestimate his powers!" he warned. "The eternal chosen one isn't dead... if he was – I would have felt it by now!"

Sorrow pushed out his black and white chest feathers and ruffled his plumage against the Hooded Crow, as they snapped their beaks together like swords. "I'm getting tired of you doubting the word of the Gullfather's elite... if you're so sure he's still alive – why don't you go and finish the job yourself!"

The Shade Runner's instinct was to back down. He had no cause to fight the Magpie. "Very well... if it's okay with Don Brando – I'll seek out Bradley Baker and destroy his legacy once and for all!"

The Gullfather agreed. "Very well, Ethan… if that's what you want to do – go and seek out this boy hero you speak of and while you're out there bring me the girl!" he chaffed and waved one of his great wings in the direction of the city. "Raith and the Magpie will oversee the connection of the pipes… I can't waste any more time here – they need me inside the statue!"

Meanwhile, the distraught Tawny Owl flew between the high-rise buildings of Lower Manhattan and used his night vision to locate the City Hall on Broadway. Jefferson spotted two more familiar birds, as described by Bradley Baker.

The Robin and the Sand Martin were speaking with a pigeon police officer and the Kingfisher. Jefferson swooped down and hooted, as he landed nearby. "Sereny… Musgrove – is that you?"

"Jefferson… thank goodness you're safe!" shouted Musgrove, as he scampered over to greet the exhausted owl.

"How did you know it was me?" asked Jefferson.

Sereny fluttered over to join them and reeped. "It's not very often you see a Tawny Owl with a baseball cap on its head!"

Jefferson looked solemn, as he reached up and wrapped his feathered fingers around the peak of the hat. "Didn't realize I still had this thing on... it's no use to me now – I look silly enough as it is!"

Musgrove insisted. "No... leave it on – it looks good on you!"

"What's wrong Jefferson?" asked Sereny, as Lieutenant Gribbon and the Kingfisher came over to find out what all the fuss was about. "Why do you look so sad?"

The owl paused to compose himself and then revealed the devastating news about the eternal chosen one. "I feel terrible... but Bradley insisted that I leave him to find King Luccese and tell him about the coin!"

"What's happened to the coin?" intervened the Lieutenant, as he unclipped a walkie-talkie from his blue police uniform.

A familiar Crossbill appeared and flew over to join Jefferson. Grog apologized for interrupting and listened intently, as the boy continued to explain the situation. "The Magpie has secured the sacred grobite and also captured Bradley... as I closed the manhole cover he was giving our friend a hell of a beating – I just hope he's okay!"

Sereny held on to Grog's midriff for comfort and swallowed deeply, as she gulped. "Where did this happen?"

The Parrot Crossbill looked on, as the dejected owl dropped his short beak and uttered. "In the sewer below East 34th Street."

Musgrove and Sereny did not hesitate and took one look at each other. "Let's go!" they chirped in unison and both took flight in the direction of the Empire State Building, quickly followed by the orange finch.

Lieutenant Gribbon excused himself from the Mayor and flew after the two young birds, as a tearful Jefferson wiped his eyes and joined the others to guide them to Bradley's underground location. The police officer clicked a button on his radio and called

Captain Sharp to give him a situation update. "Sir... the factory was empty, but we found a note stating that the Gullfather has shipped a number of containers full of Nitric Acid to Liberty Island... it's enough acid to melt the Statue of Liberty!" he cooed in a joking tone. "But seriously... I'm with the missing Crabtree boy and we're off to find Bradley – it sounds like he may be badly injured!"

A muffled crackling reply sounded out from the walkie-talkie. "Heard you loud and clear, Gribbon... glad to hear that Jefferson is safe!" replied the Captain and the questioned the Lieutenant. "I still have King Luccese, Meltor, Henley and Guan-yin here with me... they are all asking about the coin – can you confirm the Crabtree boy has the coin?"

"Negative, Sir... the Magpie has stolen the coin – it's most probably in the hands of the Gullfather by now!" There was a deathly silence, as the expected reply through the radio did not materialize. The police officer checked the device, as he struggled to fly with a single flapping wing. "Damn... I've lost the signal – I just hope they heard me!"

18

Liberty is melting!

The Hooded Crow flew down over East 34th Street and systematically assessed all the manhole covers, as he searched for clues to the whereabouts of Bradley Baker. Ethan Darke was desperate to please the Gullfather by fulfilling both tasks. He must first find his nemesis and destroy the eternal chosen one. Then he had to capture Sereny Ugbrooke and deliver her to the Statue of Liberty to complete the mysterious missing link.

The Shade Runner thought back to his time in Pathylon as the Shadow Druid's apprentice. He had relied on his stealth-like ability to instinctively evade his enemies. Now, as a blind Hooded Crow, he had to use that same skill to hunt down his prey again. It did not take him long to discover the loose manhole cover and Ethan Darke flew down to begin his descent of the metal ladder that led into the sewer.

Flaglan remained unconscious, as she lay on top of a raised ledge against the curved concrete wall of the sewer. The Sparrow Hawk's wings were badly broken and her breast heaved slowly as though her passing was imminent. The Hooded Crow strode over her limp body and he noticed a trail of blood leading to a junction up ahead. Ethan Darke bent down and ran his wing tip through the red liquid. "This isn't Sparrow Hawk blood… this belongs to a Jay – I'd say Bradley Baker is hurt pretty bad and he's nearby."

"Over here Ed-case!" shouted Bradley in a weakened voice, as he appeared from behind a pile of discarded oil drums. The injured Jay was holding his stomach and he offered the crow a chance to redeem himself. "Let's get this over with once and for all!"

"This is no contest!" replied the Shade Runner. "You are weak and the blindness you inflicted upon

198

me is no longer a hindrance… now I intend to repay you the favour by ripping out your eyes too!" He threatened. "And in the process, I'll also crush your beak into your face… so you'll also lose your sense of smell – how does that sound for starters, Baker?"

"Ethan… listen to yourself," replied Bradley in a calm tone. "You're venting your anger at me and the Gullfather is using it for his own gain… I'm sorry for what happened back in the Vortex of Silvermoor – I can't reverse what has happened but if you kill me the Gullfather wins."

The Hooded Crow cackled and cawed his unreasoned reply. "I'm passed caring about what you *or* the Gullfather thinks… your death or maiming is my main concern right now – then once I've finished with you I'll deliver the Ugbrooke girl to her certain death too!"

Bradley realized that his delay tactics were not working. He had to do something quick and he looked around the sewer for some kind of weapon. He could hear Flagan stirring and noticed her reach into her plumage, as the Hooded Crow pounced. The

Sparrow Hawk called out in pain and lifted her broken wing to throw an object towards Bradley's feet. "Ki'ki'ki… try using that!" she screamed.

Bradley bent down to try and retrieve the cutting tool that Flaglan had used to release the birds above Living Coast. The crow was too quick and knocked the wounded Jay against the wall, as he kicked the makeshift weapon into the water. Flaglan rolled off the ledge and splashed into the flowing sewage to retrieve the weapon, as Bradley fought desperately to fend off the vicious attack from the Shade Runner.

Flaglan's broken wings inhibited her attempts to locate the device but help was close at hand, as a uniformed pigeon fired a shot that ripped through one of Ethan Darke's feathered fingers. The hooded bird cawed loudly and released his hold on Bradley, as Lieutenant Gribbon was joined by Grog. The two birds jumped on top of the crow and easily overpowered the struggling Shade Runner.

Sereny and Musgrove arrived on the scene and rushed over to help their injured friend, as the Sand Martin placed her wingtip on the Jay's stomach to apply some pressure to his open wound. "That looks really bad!"

The flapping of wings echoed down the tunnel followed by a familiar hooting sound, as Jefferson appeared. "Thank goodness everyone is safe... I'm so sorry for leaving you last time, Brad!"

Bradley gasped for breath, as the deep cut in his midriff oozed more blood. "I understand, Jeffers... there was no point in you staying – anyhow, you're back now and you've brought help."

Grog and Lieutenant Gribbon continued to hold the Hooded Crow against the wall. Musgrove and Jefferson took over from Sereny, as they helped Bradley to sit down. The Sand Martin turned her back for a moment to assist Flaglan and the Shade Runner seized his opportunity. Ethan Darke mustered all his strength, as he pulled his injured wing away from the wall causing Grog to lose his balance. The Parrot Crossbill fell back into the water, as the crow followed through to swipe his wing across the weaker pigeon's beak.

"Cooooo!" cried the police officer, as the sound of breaking bones cracked and echoed through the passageways. Lieutenant Gribbon was knocked out cold and his beak hung crooked against his face.

The Hooded Crow grabbed Sereny and pulled her away from Flaglan, as he strapped a harness around the petrified Sand Martin. Ethan Darke used his rekindled stealth ability and flew at great speed along the tunnel until he reached the ladder shaft. The Shade Runner shot up through the open manhole and soared above the streets, as his distant call could be heard. "Your fate has been temporarily delayed, Baker… next time I will finish the job!"

Grog and Jefferson flew off in pursuit, while Musgrove stayed to comfort the injured birds. "What a mess… Bradley – you've lost a lot of blood!" he exclaimed and then looked over to where Flaglan was laying. "You're wings are wrecked… and we need to get Lieutenant Gribbon's beak sorted out – best get you three to the hospital!"

Back inside the Jersey Journal building, Luccese gathered Meltor, Henley, Guan-yin and Ploom together in the clock tower, as Captain Sharp continued to fiddle with the control buttons on his radio handset.

The King had heard enough, as he reluctantly took charge of the situation in a land far from his own Kingdom. He decided to address the three Pathylian High Priests and the Klomus Hawk in private. "We have to take drastic action… we have been waiting around in here for far too long and we can no longer rely on the city's pigeon police – they are getting annihilated by the Gullfather's mobster gangs!"

"What do you suggest, Sire?" asked Guan-yin, as she fluttered her green wings.

Luccese ordered the woodpecker to return to Pathylon with Ploom. "Find the Gatekeeper… Turpol will have travelled to his home in Crystal City by now and is therefore well placed to assist you in recruiting more help from Rekab!" He explained. "Then round up as many of our people in Pathylon as you can and make sure the power of flight is bestowed upon them!"

Meltor spoke. "What about Bradley Baker and Flaglan, my lord... we can't just give up on them?"

"I'm afraid they will have to fend for themselves... New York is too big a place to start searching for them now - let's just hope that Grog and the others find them alive!" insisted Luccese. "As for you, me and Henley... I suggest we head off immediately and check out the Statue of Liberty, as we originally planned before the coin was stolen – we need to find out why the Gullfather needs so much Nitric Acid and what exactly he is hiding on that island!"

Meanwhile on Liberty Island the floodlights were doused and the iconic view of the treasured symbol of justice disappeared, as Liberty's blackened image merged into the darkness of the Hudson River.

Inside the star-shaped base, the construction process was well under way beneath the statue's feet, as a hive of excited activity consumed the building. The vats of acid were safely inside and had been moved carefully into a tall-ceiling area. The pipes were connected and secured to the valves, as the hydraulic pumps were primed.

The Magpie held a lever in front of a control panel that was covered in flashing lights and he waited patiently for his boss to give the word. A flock of starlings flew across the large room and settled on perches that ran parallel with a long desk of computer screens.

The Gullfather strode his large webbed feet, as he walked awkwardly towards a pair of lift doors. Don Brando Ceeguloni stepped inside and called to his trusted henchman. "Pull the lever, Sorrow... it's time to create the greatest weapon of all time – Manhattan will revel in Liberty's new attire when the searchlights are rekindled and don't forget to press the red button to let the whole Metropolis view my creation in the making!"

The doors of the lift swished closed and the Magpie pulled the lever, as bolts of electricity sparked across the control panel. The pumps began to distribute the nitric acid into the statue and the computer screens burst into life to reveal images from cameras positioned inside the framework of the structure.

The starlings operated the remote cameras and the first pictures started to appear on the screens. They showed clear images of the specially-constructed cages that now housed some of the squawking penguin chicks. Bird technicians could be seen connecting wires to sticky pads on the *gifted and talented* children's heads. Then the Magpie pressed the red button to transmit the live images, as activity inside Liberty interrupted every broadcasting news channel across Manhattan.

Even the Kingfisher sat amazed in his City Hall chair and the Mayor stared at the TV, as the Gullfather's large yellow beak obscured one of the camera lens. The Mafia boss sat down and cleared his throat before starting to explain what was happening on Liberty Island. The Great Black-Backed Gull pulled at a purple ribbon and unravelled a piece of scrolled paper, as he read out the details of his cunning plan. "My fellow crime lords, dear residents and government officials… oh, and not forgetting our pathetic visitors from all the outside worlds they stumbled in from – I hereby offer you the opportunity to witness history in the making!" He laughed in a rough clatter. "My superior weapon will be indestructible and you will surrender Manhattan to me before daybreak… all will be revealed when the floodlights illuminate Liberty - ha'ha'ha'ha'ha-ha!"

The Mayor watched in disbelief, as the televised statement ceased momentarily and the news channels resumed their normal broadcast. "The Gullfather has gone mad… we are all in great danger – we knew he was planning some kind of weapon but I never thought the Statue of Liberty would be the symbol posing a threat to our great city!" he exclaimed and looked out of the window to witness the dawn of a new day breaking, as the sun's rays began to appear on the horizon.

One of the Kingfisher's aids adjusted the volume of the television set, as the channel flipped back to intermittent camera views inside the statue. The fuzzy images produced horrific pictures, as all 364 juvenile penguins were imprisoned inside the tiny metal pods.

Then the camera panned out to show a multitude of twisting cables that linked all the cages together. The image then switched to a much clearer outside shot and as promised, the spotlights flooded the exterior of the building.

The Kingfisher stood out of his leather chair and exclaimed. "Nothing has changed… Liberty looks just the same – no wait, look she's changing colour!"

At that moment the door of the office burst open and Captain Sharp entered. "Sorry to intrude Mr. Mayor… but I'm here to inform you that King Luccese and the High Priests have headed over to Liberty Island - the Gullfather should be captured pretty soon!"

"I take it you haven't been watching the television, Captain?" replied the Kingfisher. "Take a look at the TV… the Statue of Liberty is turning black!"

The police officer stood opened beaked, as he cooed in disgust. "She's melting… Liberty is melting – it looks like some kind of chemical reaction!"

Back on Liberty Island, the Gullfather had arrived at the crown of the statue. He was accompanied by the Magpie inside the viewing gallery, which had been transformed into a second control room. The two birds sat down to enjoy breathtaking views of Manhattan, as the sun continued to rise over the city and the outer coating of copper dissolved into the sea.

Unseen above the statue, four frustrated birds of prey hovered unable to close in because of the fumes being emitted from the toxic chemicals. King Luccese ordered Meltor and Henley to retreat, as he pointed his wing tip at the small enclosures containing the screaming penguins. "The design of those cages look familiar... they look like the one that Turpol showed us!" He declared and glanced over to indicate a nearby landing platform. "And with all that copper to melt... I can see why he needed so much Nitric Acid - we can't do anything until the chemical reaction has finished so let's land over there and wait!"

Meltor and Henley concurred, as they turned in midflight to follow their King. Their sudden change of direction was disturbed by a large flock of birds, as Henley was knocked off balance.

The disorientated Buzzard plummeted a few hundred feet before regaining his composure, as he looked up to see Meltor and Luccese battling with a group of ravens. A black-hooded bird with a mask across his beak headed out of the fracas in the direction of the crown and Henley followed in close pursuit. "That's no raven... that's a crow – and what's that thing strapped to his back?" he exclaimed and instantly recognized the reeping sound of the female bird. "Sereny... is that you?"

"Ree'reep-eep... help me, Henley – the Shade Runner is taking me to the Gullfather!" cried the helpless Sand Martin. "And Bradley is in danger... please, get someone to help him!"

Henley sped upwards to intercept the Hooded Crow and screeched in a plaintive, slightly nasal tone. He called out to the petrified Sand Martin. "Keeoow... I'm coming to get you!"

"Watch out, Henley... look behind you!" cried Sereny, as a flock of aggressive seagulls surrounded the Buzzard and scuppered his attempt to save the girl, as the Hooded Crow continued his gliding trajectory through the toxic fumes.

Henley struggled to fend off so many frantic birds and called out to Sereny again. "It's no good... there's too many of them – I can't help you!"

The Sand Martin coughed and kicked her claws against the Shade Runner's back, as she fought to release herself from the straps. "It's no use I can't get free... forget about me, Henley – go and save Bradley instead!"

Henley continued to battle with the angry birds but was still unable to gain ground on the Hooded Crow, as hundreds more seagulls appeared. They pounded the Buzzard with their squawking beaks, as he screeched out a final desperate call to the stricken female. "Where can I find Bradley?"

Sereny cleared her throat and managed to cry out one more reply. "In the sewer below East 34th Street... but hurry - he's been badly beaten and he's bleeding from the stomach!"

The Bald Eagle and the Kestrel were also struggling to fight off the ravens, as Grog and Jefferson joined them. The tawny owl hooted. "Where is Sereny?"

"You're too late!" replied Meltor. "Henley is trying to save her but it looks like Ethan Darke is taking her to the Gullfather!" cried the aging Galetian. "And we can't get anywhere near the statue without breathing apparatus... the toxic fumes created by the chemical reaction with the acid are too dangerous!"

"We can't just leave her... she'll die!" cried the Krogon.

"Sorry, Grog... we have no choice!" replied Luccese, as he grabbed two ravens and smashed their heads together. "This is useless... there's too many of them – we need to regroup!"

The three birds of prey and Crossbill had no choice but to head for Ellis Island and escape the relentless onslaught of the ravens and gulls. They retreated to regain their strength and Luccese looked up to see Henley fly off in the direction of Manhattan.

Grog enquired. "Where's he going?"

Meltor responded and fluttered his wings at a fast pace, as the Kestrel hovered to catch his breath. "His failure to save Sereny means he must be heading back to the city... let's hope he finds Bradley and the others alive!"

"We've only just left Bradley and Flaglan behind!" stated Jefferson. "Grog and I feel so guilty about leaving them in such a bad state... but someone had to go after Sereny!"

Grog added. "Let's not forget about the wounded police officer too... but I'm sure Musgrove will make sure they're all okay – hopefully he'll arrange to get them to a nearby hospital!"

Luccese appreciated their predicament. "It sounds like you had little option but leave them to follow the Sand Martin's plight... let's just hope they are okay," commiserated the King and then assessed the present situation. "There's nothing more we can do here on our own... we're going to have to sit it out until we regain our strength and get more help!" stated the Bald Eagle, as they watched the Statue of Liberty complete its amazing transformation.

19

In a Coma

At the crown of the Statue, Ethan Darke continued to hold the gas mask over his beak and flew through one of the open windows. Don Brando Ceeguloni could not believe his eyes, as the Hooded Crow entered the control room. The Shade Runner had managed to fulfill his promise by capturing the last piece the gull needed to complete his giant puzzle.

The 365th cage had already been installed in the crown and was ready to receive Sereny Ugbrooke, as she struggled to free herself. The window was closed and the Sand Martin breathed more easily, as Sorrow released her from the crows back. The Magpie quickly secured her inside the last cage, as the Gullfather gave the order for the female's brain to be connected to the statue. A starling technician chirped excitedly and proceeded to attach the sticky pads to either side of her feathered head, as a switch was turned to supply a small current of electricity.

The Hooded Crow held his injured wing by his side and enquired. "What now, Don Brando?"

The Gullfather removed the gold coin from his jacket pocket and asked the Magpie to place it into a round recess in the desk, as a TV monitor displayed a panoramic view of the melting statue in full. "Watch this… you're going to be very impressed with the outcome – ha'ha'ha'ha'ha!"

A short distance away in Manhattan, Henley flew past the Empire State Building and soon arrived over East 34th Street. Flashing blue lights illuminated the street, as a group of pigeon police secured yellow tape around the area where the manhole cover had been dislodged.

The Buzzard flew down and landed next to the officer in charge. "What's going on?" he enquired, as an ambulance sped off with its sirens screaming.

"One of our guys is badly hurt… they've just taken him to the hospital in that ambulance - a Jay and a Sparrow Hawk are travelling with him and they looked pretty bashed up too!" shouted the police officer, as a line of yellow-taxis queued bumper-to-bumper down the busy street. The cab drivers tooted their horns in an annoying defiance of the road-block. "A young Robin is travelling with them too!" declared the pigeon, as the noise of the horns reached a deafening pitch.

"Thanks… that means Bradley, Flaglan and Muzzy are in the vehicle with Lieutenant Gribbon – I'd better get after them!" replied Henley and dipped his hunched neck, as he spread out his broad wings.

The Buzzard fluttered his wing tips and projected his muscular body off the ground, as the short-feathered tail guided him over the queues of stranded taxi cabs. He soared along at great speed with his wings raised in a shallow V-shape and soon caught up with the emergency vehicle. Henley's huge frame landed heavily on the flashing blue lights and the agile bird swung round to kick open the rear doors of the ambulance.

Musgrove instinctively stood and spread out his wings to shield the three unconscious patients. The Robin instantly recognised the Buzzard and breathed a sigh of relief. "Thank goodness it's you, Henley... I thought the Hooded Crow had come back!"

"Nah, I'm afraid he's eluded us all... he's now back with *psycho-gull* and the Magpie - they've got Sereny secured in the Statue of Liberty!" replied the Buzzard. "You should see what the Gullfather has built... he's totally converted the statue and positioned a load of caged penguin's inside the limbs of the statue – even the outer skin of copper has totally melted away!"

"Did you say penguins?" asked Musgrove.

"Yes... why?" replied Henley.

"Doesn't matter... it's a Batman joke!" quirked the Robin, as he ruffled his bright red plumage. "Bradley and Sereny would understand!"

Henley dismissed Musgrove's super hero quip, as he shook his head to ruffle the feathers around his broad neck. The Buzzard then focussed his attention on two bulky long-tailed Whitethroats dressed in green uniforms. "Hi there… I hadn't noticed you there – I'm, errrr related to the Jay!" he explained, as the two paramedics afforded the bird of prey a disbelieving look. "Yeah… err – difficult to imagine isn't it!"

Musgrove turned to lean over his injured friend and repositioned the oxygen mask that covered Bradley's beak. "The paramedics have managed to stabilize Flaglan and Lieutenant Gribbon… but Bradley's health is critical – he's lost a lot of blood and he keeps slipping in and out of a coma!"

The monitoring equipment connected to the Jay started to beep loudly, as the graph on the small screen flat-lined. The paramedics maneuvered their bulky long tails past the Robin and grabbed a resuscitation pack with their broad rusty-brown feathered fingers.

The ambulance moved from side to side, as the batteries charged and the Whitethroats took it in turns to pound the Jay's chest. The equipment beeped again and the paramedics asked everyone to stand clear, as they held the metal pads in position.

THUD! The Jay's upper body jolted and the line on the graph spiked sharply, as the peaks steadied to a normal pulse. One of Whitethroats explained the seriousness of Bradley's condition. "He won't survive another scare like that... he's lost too much blood!" Diagnosed the paramedic. "He is going to need a blood transfusion as soon as we get to the hospital... or he will die – we will need to contact his parents because the tests show he has a very rare blood group!"

Henley gulped. "His parents will be of no use!"

Musgrove responded. "But surely one of us can go back through the time portal and bring them here... we still have time – I don't mind going now!"

"Stop!" ordered Flaglan, as the Sparrow Hawk regained consciousness. "That's not what Henley meant, Muzzy!"

The Buzzard lowered his hooked beak. He knew the time had come for him to reveal the deep secret he had been hiding from Bradley. "Flaglan is right, Muzzy... Margaret and Patrick will not be able to help."

"But they will have the same blood group as Bradley... we need at least one of them here if he's going to survive – the paramedic said he has a very rare blood group!" insisted Musgrove.

Flaglan's broken wings prevented her from moving off the bed so she summoned Musgrove by flicking her head. "Come over here, Muzzy... Henley and I have something to tell you but you must not repeat anything we say to Bradley – do you understand?"

The Robin did not answer and simply nodded, as the emergency vehicle sped along 5th Avenue until it reached the entrance to the hospital. Henley perched himself next to Musgrove and tried to explain the life-changing news about Bradley's true identity. The conversation was halted abruptly, as the rear doors of the ambulance opened and Henley promised. "I will tell you everything... once we are inside the hospital!"

Meanwhile on Liberty Island, the Gullfather puffed on his cigar and pressed more buttons on the illuminated control panel inside the crown. The coin had now been fully activated and the green copper that had once coated the Statue of Liberty had completely dissolved. The great monument still retained its iconic shape with a skeletal framework of forged metal connecting the lightweight metal cages.

The toxic gases had dispersed and posed no further threat to the crew, as the gangsters removed the gas masks from their beaks. Don Brando Ceeguloni, Sorrow and the Ethan Darke had now been joined by Raith, as the four mobsters instigated the next stage of Liberty's transformation.

The Gullfather chewed the end of his cigar and declared. "At last... all 365 cages are connected as one - with the brain of Sereny Ugbrooke linking the gifted and talented school children to the crown's main power unit!"

The Hooded Crow sat back in one of the chairs and tipped the end of his trilby hat, as he cawed a favourable retort. "I am proud to be part of your evil plan, Don Brando... and I'm looking forward to the next stage!"

"And I am glad you decided to join my quest to wreak havoc across New York... and now you are about to witness Liberty leaving her island prison forever!" squawked the Gullfather, as he pushed the coin deeper into the recess and a flashing laser-bolt shot out from the end of the statue's raised arm. "Good... it appears the arm is fully functional... the damaged caused by the blast from Black Tom has been repaired – the torch is in good working order!"

Another laser fired from the torch and Raith cawed in admiration. "The laser is not as strong as you anticipated, boss!"

"Silence... you fool!" shouted the great Black-Backed Gull. "Once we are disconnected from the power source in the base below... we will need to reach our intended destination within fifteen minutes before the batteries drain – then you will see what the torch is really capable of!"

"Oh, I see… so where are you taking us, boss?" asked the quivering Raven.

"To a more elevated position of course… where we can control the whole of Manhattan and destroy many worlds far away from here – including Pathylon!" replied the deluded gull, as he ordered the Magpie to pull another a lever on the control panel.

The young penguins struggled inside their cages and squawked, as the power passed through their brains to control the movement of each giant limb. The statue's legs lifted clear of the base and the crashing sound of broken mortar showered the nearby wooden pier. The rest of the debris landed in the surrounding water causing mini-tsunami's to smash against the shores of Lower Manhattan. The creaking of twisted metal produced a chilling rendition, as the statue detached herself from the island and stepped into the river. The power lit the eye sockets of the huge transparent statue and they glowed red, as Liberty began her journey across the Hudson.

20

The Foundling

The Kingfisher and Captain Sharp were transfixed to a large plasma screen in the Mayor's office, as they watched the city's emergency defense squads in action. They had ordered pigeon police S.W.A.T. teams to gather along the shoreline of Lower Manhattan, whilst *Sikorsky* army helicopters circled the crown of the vibrant Statue of Liberty.

King Luccese, Meltor, Grog and Jefferson had been resting on the nearby Ellis Island and were now fully recovered from their previous battles. The Pathylon trio and the Tawny Owl rejoined the airborne assault, as noisy Oystercatcher photographers carrying cameras flew close by.

The aerial pictures were being broadcast live via the antenna at the top of the Empire State Building and the signal strength increased, as the animated statue waded its way across the water from Liberty Island.

The monument's amazing transformation was also being broadcast on television monitors inside the hospital where Bradley Baker had been taken. The eternal chosen one's eyes remained closed, as the Jay was stretchered out of the ambulance and into the building on 5th Avenue. The first of three stretchers were wheeled through the main entrance, as Musgrove and Henley fluttered close behind. The end of Bradley's bed smashed into the doors, as the activity inside the busy A & E department burst into life. The severity of the young Jay's statistics were checked and confirmed with the paramedics before he was rushed straight through to the operating theatres.

Henley looked up at one of the screens and groaned. "The Gullfather's creation is heading for Manhattan… and look – there is King Luccese and

Meltor!" keeoowed the Buzzard. "I have to get back and help them… but first I need to help Bradley!"

Musgrove looked up at the monitor to view the familiar Tawny Owl and the Crossbill's frantic efforts to keep up with the other birds of prey, as the camera lens panned in on Grog's flapping orange wings. The Robin then afforded the High Priest a confused look. "What do you mean by *help Bradley*?"

Henley chose to ignore the question, as he entered a small rest room where Flaglan had been taken. Musgrove followed the Buzzard and tried to converse again but Henley completed a U-turn and pushed past the frustrated Robin. The reluctant High Priest politely excused himself and made his way down the corridor to where Bradley was being prepped.

"Where is Henley going?" asked Musgrove, as he looked over to the afflicted Sparrow Hawk. "Why didn't he answer me… why didn't he confirm why Patrick and Margaret Baker's blood would be of no use - how can *he* possibly help Bradley?"

Flaglan readjusted her position on the bed and asked Musgrove to move the pillows, as the Robin obliged. "Thank you… that's much better… so many questions – now here's the reason why." The Sparrow Hawk composed herself and continued. "Henley is feeling very emotional right now and it's very understandable why he is acting this way," she explained. "Patrick and Margaret Baker are not the boy's bloodline parents… Bradley was adopted as a baby – the eternal chosen one is a *foundling* and is not from your world!"

Musgrove looked confused. "What's a *foundling*?"

Flaglan explained. "A baby that has been abandoned by its mother… a baby that is taken into care by others."

Musgrove was stunned to hear such shocking news and did not stay to hear the Sparrow Hawk continue. The Robin headed out of the room and took flight, as he flew swiftly along the hospital's corridors. He reached the reception area outside the operating theatres and spotted Bradley's bed.

Henley was stroking the Jay's brow. "Hello Musgrove… sorry for rushing off like that – I was worried about Bradley."

"Get away from him… you liar – get your filthy talons off my friend!" shouted Musgrove.

Henley paused for a moment, as Flaglan's bed appeared along the corridor. The Sparrow Hawk had been wheeled down in pursuit of the frantic Robin, as the Buzzard looked over to his fellow High Priestess for support.

The Sparrow Hawk nodded and assured Henley it was the right time to tell Musgrove the whole truth. The Buzzard then asked. "How much have you told him?"

Before Flaglan could respond, Musgrove continued his discourse upon hearing of their deception against his friend. "I've heard enough to know that when Bradley wakes he will be devastated… when he finds out about his true identity – it will be like his parents have suddenly died!" He declared. "His heart will feel like it's been ripped from his chest… and as you are well aware, I know how that feels - it happened to me for real when I killed my own father, the Shadow Druid!"

Flaglan tried to calm the young Robin and explained that Bradley's so-called uncle had meant no harm by keeping the boy's real identity a secret. "Henley was under strict orders from King Luccese and Meltor not to say anything after you helped release his soul from the Vortex of Silvermoor... not wanting to tell Bradley the truth was the main reason he stayed behind in Pathylon to assume the role of High Priest to the Devonians – he didn't really want to be apart from his S....!"

Musgrove interrupted at a crucial point and reacted angrily. "I can't believe you all thought that Bradley would never find out... he was allowed to keep the coin so was bound to return at some point – Henley must have known he would eventually have to tell Bradley that he was adopted!"

Flaglan cast the Buzzard a cruel stare. "I'm sick of defending you, Henley... you should be explaining your own actions, not me!"

Musgrove kept moving his head from side to side, as if was watching a game of tennis. He looked between Henley and Flaglan for more clarification and the Buzzard remained silent.

The frustrated Sparrow Hawk attempted to move one of her broken wings. "Ki'ki'ki-ki-ki... you are a coward, Henley!" She cried and decided to continue her stubborn defense of the silent Buzzard. "Henley had no choice but to hide Bradley's true identity... remember, as a High Priest he was under strict orders - he didn't think Bradley would ever need to know!" She explained and then paused, as she changed tact. "It's good that the eternal chosen one has returned to help us rid our world of the Gullfather's threat and it's unfortunate that he sustained such a life-threatening injury – but think about it, maybe we should be concentrating on the productive things that could develop from all this!"

"What are you suggesting?" asked Henley, as he finally broke his silence.

"I'd like us to take a different view on these unfortunate circumstances," replied Flaglan.

Henley quickly read into what the sorceress was inferring. "No Flaglan... we can't – we have to tell Bradley the truth!"

Flaglan responded. "Think about it, Henley... he's in a coma – he doesn't need to know anything!"

Henley reacted angrily and shouted. "It didn't take long for your evil side to raise its ugly head again... I assume you are you suggesting that we try to keep the secret from Bradley?"

"Yes... for now – or at least until our safe return to Pathylon after Luccese and Meltor have sorted out this stupid Gullfather business!" replied Flaglan.

Henley reacted in a defensive manner. "That's an absurd suggestion, Flaglan... you should be ashamed of yourself – I intend to tell Bradley the truth as soon as he wakes up!"

Musgrove had calmed slightly and watched the two Pathylian High Priests continue to argue at his friend's expense. Something else had been playing on his mind and he interrupted to ask the flustered Sparrow Hawk a question. "If all this is true and you were so keen to keep his true identity a secret… why was Bradley allowed to keep the coin?"

Flaglan looked shocked, as she composed herself and replied. "He didn't keep the coin!"

"Yes he did!" insisted Musgrove.

Henley confirmed Flaglan's retort. "What she means is that Jefferson took it from Bradley on purpose when you all returned home last time… he was supposed to protect the coin – that's why he returned to America with his parents *and the coin*!"

"You mean Jefferson has been in on this secret all along?" yelled Musgrove.

"Please, Muzzy… keep your voice down – I promise you that everything will make more sense when you know the whole truth," chirped the Buzzard.

"I've had enough of all this nonsense!" shouted Musgrove and he headed for a nearby toilet.

"No, Muzzy... wait - don't go!" shouted Henley, as the bathroom door slammed shut.

Musgrove had grown tired of all the charades and turned the taps on the hand basin, as he flushed his red facial feathers and stared at his bird-like reflection in the mirror. "This isn't happening... it's all a nightmare and I'm going to wake up any minute!" he cried and fluttered the ends of his wings across his wet face. "Come on... wake up – wake up Musgrove!"

The door to the bathroom opened slightly and Flaglan hooked her speckled head around the gap. "Ki'ki'ki-ki, are you okay in there, Muzzy... please come out – I'm sorry for suggesting what I did."

Musgrove wiped his face with a paper towel and walked over to the apologetic Sparrow Hawk. "You're forgiven!" He smiled and walked out of the room. He hopped across the corridor to where Bradley was being prepared for his operation and noticed Henley still standing by the strickened Jay's bed. He puffed out his red breast in a protective manner and demanded to know what the Buzzard was doing. "Henley... Flaglan has just apologized but I now want you to tell me the whole truth and why you have got tubes sticking out of your wing!"

Henley called Musgrove over to Bradley's side and placed his finger-like wing tips on the young Robin's shoulders. "Please sit down, Muzzy… I'm sorry too – now let me explain what I'm about to do."

"Well… go on – I'm listening!" replied Musgrove, as his calmed demeanor soon changed to frustration again. "Come on Henley… I can't stand this much longer – tell me!" cried the Robin.

"Muzzy… I'm just about to donate blood - I am trying to help Bradley to live."

"But your blood is worthless… the paramedic said Bradley has a rare blood type – only his real mother or father can give him blood!" insisted Musgrove, as he held his head in his wings. The Robin then lifted his beak slowly to reveal his crying eyes. "No… you can't be – you are *the foundling's* real father!"

A senior nurse rushed over to stop Musgrove from falling down, as the Robin feinted and the matron insisted that everyone calm down. "The patient is still in a coma… you are just making matters worse by shouting – now, please let us do our job and transfuse the blood that he desperately needs."

Smelling salts were wafted beneath Musgrove's beak and he soon recovered, as he held his head in his wings again. He watched Bradley laying very still on the bed, as a sharp needle was pushed beneath the Jay's feathers. Anesthetic entered the tubes to ensure the boy's slumber before Henley's blood began to flow into his body.

Flaglan looked around the side of the attending nurse and noticed one of Bradley's eyelids flicker, as a tear rolled down the side of the Jay's face. The Sparrow Hawk took a deep breath, as Bradley appeared to react to the effects of the anesthetic. The sorceress took another sharp intake of breath and then declared. "I think he heard us... I believe the eternal chosen one is aware of his true identity!"

Musgrove lifted his head and offered a scowling glance in Henley direction, as he warned the Buzzard. "You'd better prepare yourself for when *your Son* wakes up... Bradley Baker is going to be one very *angry bird*!"

21

Eagle Wings

The pair of heavy doors that fronted the Mayor's office inside City Hall burst open, as a tall scrawny bird marched through unannounced. The large white Heron was quickly followed by a squadron of uniformed soldiers that filtered off either side to form a protective circle around the circumference of the room.

The geese-like regiment stood to attention, as the long beak of the commanding officer turned like the jib of a crane. The intimidating river-bird scanned the startled officials inside the office, as he pushed past a government aid to stand in front of the Mayor's large polished desk. "I'll be needing that seat Mr. Mayor!"

The startled Kingfisher stood out of his seat and shouted in disgust. "What is the meaning of this... how dare you burst into my office without permission?"

"Permission!" grumbled the intimidating army officer, as he removed his green beret to reveal a cap of red feathers. "I don't need permission... I am General Crade!"

Captain Sharp stepped forward to confront the high-ranked soldier. "First King Luccese and now you... just how many wannabe heroes intend to undermine our efforts to stop the Gullfather?"

The General pushed the pigeon away with his long white wing and uttered his response. "You need to get back to the pathetic seaside town you flew in from and stick to dealing with petty thieves... this is New York City – a city that never sleeps and I'm about to give the Gullfather a wakeup call!" He shouted and pointed to the large plasma TV screen. "Watch and learn how the professionals get rid of Mafia scum!"

Captain Sharp and the Kingfisher stared at the television to witness a unit of ten heavily armed helicopters flying in a v-shaped formation towards the statue. It was very clear that the government officials were no longer in charge of the city's defenses. The pelican pilots flying the helicopters had been instructed by the General to fire at the statue as soon as they were in range.

The Mayor covered his mouth and muttered to the police officer. "It would appear General Crade has now officially taken over command inside City Hall... we don't have much choice - there's not much we can do about those things."

Meanwhile, the converted statue continued to wade through the deep water of the Hudson, as it moved sluggishly towards the skyscrapers on the horizon. The brain-power from the innocent minds of the gifted and talented children was being harnessed, as the huge structure repelled the missiles being fired from the helicopter gunships.

Luccese was not helping the ally's cause, as the Bald Eagle swooped down to grab the missiles in midflight. Meltor could see why the King was scuppering the attack, as the Kestrel flew down to join Grog and Jefferson in close formation.

The Gullfather was intrigued at the bravery displayed by the eagle and pleased that the heroic bird of prey was prepared to defend his giant creation. But the King was not helping either side and Meltor encouraged the Crossbill and the Tawny Owl to remind the mob leader of their true allegiance, as they pointed their sharp talons at the statue's crown.

Back inside City Hall, the Kingfisher pleaded with General Crade to stop firing at the statue. "There are school kids in that thing... we have to stop the Gullfather some other way!"

Crade ignored the Mayor and continued to watch the television screen, as the four allies maintained their inadvertent defense of the moving statue. The frustrated Heron exclaimed. "What are those damn birds from Pathylon doing... they're gonna get themselves and my troops killed – why are they protecting the Gullfather?"

Captain Sharp stepped forward and reiterated the Mayor's request. "Can't you see… they are defending the penguin chicks and Sereny Ugbrooke - you have to stop firing your missiles!"

The army commander paused and mirrored the great gull inside Liberty by striking a match and lighting a fat cigar. "Very well… we'll try and find another way!" he quipped, as his long pointed beak crashed together and compressed the smoking tobacco. Crade grunted in exasperation and turned to one of his lieutenants. "Radio the pelican's… tell them to cease fire – for now!"

The Gullfather ignored the ongoing battle in the skies above the crown. Don Brando Ceeguloni was more concerned about the statue's slow progress through the water. The strong undercurrent was not helping the situation and he stared at the power status of the fuel cells. "It has taken over ten minutes to get this far... the batteries are draining too fast – we only have five more minutes to reach our destination!"

"What do you suggest, boss?" asked Raith.

"Push that green button to your left!" squawked the Gullfather. "We shall impress the viewing public and government officials even further with more features on my incredible new toy... the Kingfisher will be very impressed with my next trick - activate Liberty's wings!"

Sereny Ugbrooke's eyes opened, as a strong electrical current ran through the metal cage that secured her slender frame. The Sand Martin's body became rigid and her panoramic view from inside the crown of the statue allowed the frightened girl to see the cityscape ahead.

Raith kept his wing tips firmly pressed on the green button, as the Gullfather turned in his seat to stare up at the suspended cage. He laughed and called up to Sereny. "Your wings are about to help Liberty take to the skies... you were purposely placed in the brain of my great creation because you are the *Golden Girl* – now you will turn into a magnificent *Golden Eagle* and your strength will elevate us to a new vantage point!"

The Hooded Crow cackled. "Where will the girl's eagle wings take us?"

Don Brando Ceeguloni turned to face Manhattan and pointed to an iconic tower in the centre of the city. "There, my dear Ethan... to the Empire State Building!" he squawked, as the power increased and the cage holding the Sand Martin began to reform.

Sereny's body increased in size dramatically and the colour of her plumage changed to the distinctive dark brown feathers of the great bird of prey. A golden nape appeared and her broader wings shot out from either side of the cage, as a ripple of energy forced her resplendent feathers outwards.

The energy was replicated on Liberty's upper-back, as an opening appeared on the metal spine of the statue. The golden girl's movements were being simulated and the cables connecting her mind to the control room transferred power to a set of golden feathered wings that began to emerge from the gap in the statue's skeletal frame.

King Luccese had been watching the next stage of transformation, as he flew majestically around the back of the statue. He stared in amazement, as the pair of giant eagle wings emerged from between Liberty's shoulder blades and he called over to Meltor. "Retreat... there's something really weird happening to the back of the statue – it appears to have the ability to fly!"

The Kestrel pulled back and hovered, as Jefferson and Grog followed Meltor's lead. They heeded the King's warning and the three birds joined Luccese. They flew away from the creaking monument, as the enormous wings fully developed.

Luccese shouted. "We may have stopped the army from firing their missiles but there's nothing more we can do to prevent that thing from taking to the air... the statue is getting stronger and more agile by the minute!"

Grog called over to the King. "What do you suggest we do... we can't fire at the penguins and we do not have the strength to overcome the metal monster!"

Luccese turned to Meltor and offered his faithful High Priest a defeated stare. "We have no choice... we must head for the Met Life clock tower - I think it's time we headed back to Pathylon to get more help!"

Jefferson interrupted. "But surely Guan-yin and Ploom will have done that... don't you trust them?"

The King nodded. "Of course I trust them... but time is moving on and they must be struggling to find Turpol - they should have returned by now!"

Meltor concurred. "I agree, my lord...our efforts are best served by re-entering the time portal and returning to our homeland – Guan-yin needs help!"

The pressure on Sereny's brain was becoming insufferable and she screamed in pain, as the giant mechanical limbs completed their wingspan. The Gullfather puffed on his cigar and lifted a feathered finger. "I think I should stop now... I don't want the golden girl to die just yet – I will be needing more of her brain-power to lift Liberty to her lofty perch in the sky!"

Meanwhile King Luccese led Meltor, Jefferson and Grog away from the menacing statue, as they flew in the direction of Manhattan. The apex of the illuminated Met Life tower structure appeared in the distance. Its familiar four clock faces, one on each side of the building, were located from the 25th to 27th floor. The gilded cupola at the very top of the building served as an 'eternal light' which guided the weary birds to the top of its spire.

At last they landed safely on some ornate balustrades that edged the peaked roof and Jefferson was quick to enquire about the clock faces. "This may be a coincidence… but I can't help but notice that all the time portals linked to New York seem be located beneath some kind of clock tower."

Meltor interpreted the owl's curiosity. "It's no coincidence, Jefferson… the clocks do bear an important relevance to our mission – they are all operating concurrent with the same time dimension, which means that the entrance to each time portal will close at an exact set moment in time!"

King Luccese concurred with the wise old Galetian's explanation. "Meltor is right... unfortunately our time here is limited!" confirmed the Bald Eagle. "Each vortex entrance is controlled by the clocks and they need to have time constraints or they would all implode... when the hands on all the clocks in New York move to eleven o'clock this morning – the time portals beneath them all will close forever!"

The revelation of the regulated time schedule struck a chord and hastened the King's determination to get back to Pathylon for help, as he circled the top of the Met Life clock tower. Luccese spotted an opening and signalled to the others to follow his lead, as they flew one-by-one through a vent cowl on the roof. The protective cover led to the top of an elevator shaft and the birds hovered over the vertical drop, as they waited for the rising elevator to stop.

Meltor turned his grey speckled body sideways and shot passed the stationary lift car, as the others followed his trajectory down the deep shaft that led to the basement.

Grog looked down and offered some words of advice to Jefferson, as the updraft increased the force against their beaks. The Crossbill narrowed his eyes and squawked his warning. "Remember to keep your wings back and just keep heading down… and don't stop when you reach the bottom – just keep going!"

Luccese had the superior speed and passed the leading Kestrel, as the solid floor neared. The Bald Eagle aimed his great yellow beak downwards, as he thrust his wings backwards. "Let's get back to Pathylon!" He exclaimed, as the bottom of the shaft opened to reveal a swirling abyss beneath.

Jefferson closed his eyes, as he followed the other three birds into the time portal and their resulting entry into the vortex produced a flash of lightning that shot upwards. The energy force from the blast created a recurrent effect along the lift cables, as the backdraft of a giant fireball escaped through the top of the skyscraper into the early morning sky.

22

Downfall

Henley stared out of the hospital window that faced the distant Met Life clock tower, as the exploding light created an illuminating display. The Buzzard felt a chilling sense of fear, as he uttered. "That was a huge flash and it could only mean one thing... a powerful force has re-entered the vortex," he confirmed. "A display of that magnitude indicates that King Luccese must be returning to Pathylon... it means the Gullfather's creation must have the power to cause even greater harm than we first thought!"

Musgrove appeared by Henley's side and looked out to see what was attracting the Buzzard's attention.

"Wow... that's one hell of a blast!" exclaimed the Robin.

Henley turned away and walked slowly towards the recovery room where Bradley was sleeping. He stared through a viewing panel at the helpless Jay and revealed his fears. "Bradley is going to wake up and find a New York that is in great danger... without the coin, he will be unable the enact the duty bestowed upon – his role as *the eternal chosen one* to defend Pathylon will be rendered useless, never mind his ability to stop the Gullfather."

The Buzzard opened the door to the recovery room and entered, as Musgrove followed. The Robin cleared his throat and asked. "Aren't you forgetting something much more important... what about Bradley's reaction when he wakes up to find out about his true identity – what's he going to say when he finds out you're his real Dad?"

"I already know," whispered the Jay in a weak voice. "I heard everything."

Henley reacted in a nervous fashion and he rushed over to kneel at Bradley's bedside. "I am so sorry...

we thought you were unconscious - the nurses and paramedics told us you were in a coma!"

Bradley tried to sit up but he was still too weak. "Well you were wrong and now I know everything… I have been lying here contemplating what to do – should I react in an angry manner or just accept the truth and get on with it."

Musgrove asked his friend. "And what have you decided?"

Bradley paused and stared at the two horns sticking out of the feathers on Henley's head, as he replied very calmly. "I already knew you were my real father from the first time I looked into your empty face… during our time together in Silvermoor, the Mauled Miner showed me great kindness and a deep feeling of love – something I have never felt before, not even from my parents back home."

Tears began to well up in Henley's eyes and he held out his wing to the understanding Jay. "Everything is going to be okay, Son… I promise!"

Bradley choked and his voice broke under the emotional strain, as he managed to compose himself.

"I am the eternal chosen one... I still have the power to help defeat the evil that threatens this city – I know there's lots more to discuss about how I deal with finding out about my true identity but first we must find the sacred grobite and stop the Gullfather!"

Henley anticipated a question that Bradley was bound to ask. "Don't you want to know who your real Mother is?"

"Yes, of course I do... but as I said - now is not the time and we cannot abandon our mission!" replied Bradley, as he mustered the strength to sit upright.

Musgrove cheered. "Bradley Baker you are an incredible person... a great hero and I'm privileged to be here to fight at your side!"

"Thanks Muzzy!" responded the resilient Jay, as his recovery showed strong signs of improvement. "And please be assured... whatever anger I do have inside me, it will be directed at the Gullfather and Ethan Darke - so let's get out there and kick some serious bird butt!"

Back on board the Statue of Liberty, the Gullfather ordered the golden girl's brain to be utilized to full affect as the Magpie pulled another lever and more buttons were pressed on the control panel. The ear-piercing sound of creaking metal resonated through the structure and the metal skeleton lifted out of the Hudson, as the enormous wings flapped profusely. Liberty soared into the air and raised her wings into a V-shape, as the airborne statue glided towards the Empire State Building.

Sorrow struggled to control the great machine and began to panic, as he let go of the throttle. The frantic Magpie stood out of his seat and declared. "The batteries are almost empty... we are about to lose power to the cages – if we don't land this thing soon..."

"Shut up and sit back down... you insolent bird-thief – now strap yourself in over there!" squawked the cigar smoking Gangster, as he ordered the Magpie to step aside. "I'll take the controls from here... this is going to be a piece of cake!" He boasted, as the statue soared higher into the air and circled the antenna at the top of the building.

The Hooded Crow and Raith stayed silent, as Sorrow sulked in the corner. They watched with baited breath, as the Gullfather guided the statue directly above the antenna and Ethan Darke could not resist asking if he could complete the task. "I would be most honoured, Don Brando if you could allow me to help."

The Gullfather hesitated then stood out of the seat. "Very well... she's all yours, Ethan - I believe when the account of my great achievement is recorded in New York's history books, the fact that a Shade Runner helped to land Liberty on top of the Empire State Building will make excellent reading!"

"Thank you!" replied the Hooded Crow and took the controls, as the Gullfather walked over to the viewing gallery. "Where are you going, Don Brando?"

"Over there, to the 86th floor... I need to access the observatory and isolate the upper floors to prevent any intruders entering the roof of the Empire State

Building!" replied the great gull. "We will also need to secure the broadcasting station at the top of the tower so you can come with me!" he insisted, as he pointed to Sorrow. "Go down to the *'Great Book'* and assemble a flock of starlings... then meet me in the broadcasting station once Liberty has docked on top of the antenna - we have to ensure the power to her batteries is maintained so the weapon can be fired!"

The dawn was entering its final phase, as the sun rose higher over Manhattan. The trembling Magpie disappeared out of the crown and made his way down the narrow spiral staircase inside the Statue's body to the stone tablet that was still being held in Liberty's left hand. A group of fifty-or-so starlings were congregated on the book waiting for further orders. Sorrow approached the flock and delivered the Gullfather's request, as they flew away from the statue creating a swirling black mass in the early morning sky.

Back inside the Mayor's office the Kingfisher had managed to calm the situation and General Crade moved out of his desk chair. The military leader was now commanding the allied attack using a large boardroom table as a makeshift model to enact a simulation of his battle plan.

The Heron used a broom handle to push a pile of reference books to the centre of the table, as a desk lamp was positioned on top to mimic the Statue of Liberty. "My elite pelican pilots report that the statue, depicted here by the lamp... is being docked on top of the Empire State Building!" He continued to procrastinate, as he explained the table layout. "I've decided to use a stack of the Mayor's collection of tourism books to act as the skyscraper!"

Captain Sharp interrupted and confirmed the helicopter pilot's communication, as he pointed to the television screen. "Why don't we just watch it on TV... all the news channels are covering the action well enough to see what's going on out there, General – the live images are just showing the base of the statue completing its connection with the top of the Empire State Building!"

"Mmmm!" mumbled the red crested Heron. "Ahhh yes, well... ermmmm – okay, forget the table lamp and the books then!" Retorted the embarrassed army officer, as he clicked a button on his radio. "Yankee, Yankee... one niner – come in one niner!"

A crackled voice replied from inside one of the helicopters, as it circled the fixed statue. "One niner here, Sir... the Gullfather and the Magpie have been sighted flying into the observatory on the 86th floor of the Empire State Building – shall we open fire on them?"

The General looked over to Captain Sharp and the Kingfisher for their reaction, as they both shook their heads in disbelief. Crade's facial white feathers reddened to match his crested quill and returned his instruction to the helicopter pilot. "That's a negative one niner... hold your fire and keep a safe distance – the penguin kids are still connected inside the statue and your missiles could also destabilize the top of the building!"

Captain Sharp spoke over the General's communication with his pilots and released a cry of relief, as the TV camera's homed in on three familiar birds arriving at the top of the Empire State Building.

Bradley Baker and Henley flew ahead with Musgrove trailing slightly behind the stronger birds. They had left Flaglan and Lieutenant Gribbon behind at the hospital, where their injuries were being taken care of by the hospital staff. The three determined birds began to circle the observatory, as Don Brando Ceeguloni and Sorrow looked out to see the Jay's determined face. Bradley called out to the over-confident Mafia boss. "We are here to take you down, Gullfather!"

"Ha'ha'ha-ha... what can a *titchy blue jaybird* do to stop me and my magnificent machine from destroying New York?" teased the gull. "Fly away little bird and take your sidekick Robin with you... and here's a message for your Buzzard friend too – buzz off!"

Bradley ignored the Gullfather's taunts and flew down to land at the statue's feet, as Henley and Musgrove perched nearby. There was a loud whirling sound inside the statue and a bolt of power surged from the antenna to recharge batteries. The energy filtered through the fledgling penguins to feed the statue's raised arm, as a laser beam shot out of the torch.

The startled Robin quickly realized. "So that's why he needed the sacred grobite so badly… to trigger the torch!"

Henley nodded and spotted an enraged look on the Gullfather's reddened face. "Yeah… but looking at *psycho-gulls* reaction - it would appear the laser has been activated too soon!"

Bradley looked on intently as the helicopter gunships reacted offensively by firing their missiles at the powerful beam being discharged from the torch in Liberty's hand. He then moved his head slightly and followed the skeletal arm, as he stopped his line of vision at the elbow. The Jay had noticed something sticking out of the joint and shouted over to Henley. "Look over there… I've spotted something!"

The Buzzard followed the direction of Bradley's pointing wing but before he could react, Musgrove spied a large black and white bird flying away from the observatory. "Hey look, Brad... it's our feathered friend again – the one that stole all the children from Devon!"

Sorrow panicked, as he escaped the military bombardment from the helicopters and the Gullfather shouted at his fleeing henchman. "Get back here you coward!" The petrified Magpie turned to witness another raging expression across the face of his boss and it was the last image he saw before his *downfall*, as a missile hit his midriff. The resulting explosion filled the air with a cloud of bloodstained feathers and Don Brando Ceeguloni sniggered, as the remains of the dead gangster fell to the streets below. "That will teach you to fly away... you idiot!"

The helicopter pilots received orders to cease firing their missiles, as Bradley took advantage of the silence to repeat his observation to Henley and Musgrove. "I've definitely spotted a flaw in the statue's design... there could be a way to stop the Gullfather's creation!"

22

Angel of the Waters

Meanwhile a few hours earlier in Pathylon, the entrance to the time portal in the Unknown Land swirled, as Luccese and Meltor waited nearby for Guan-yin to arrive. The King was hoping that the Hartopian High Priestess had managed to visit all five regions and recruit the reinforcements he needed to make the journey back to New York.

Jefferson was delighted to be back to is normal self, as the boy adjusted his baseball cap and held out his hands. He wiggled his fingers and looked over to where Grog was standing. "How does it feel to lose the orange feathers?"

The Krogon grunted and shrugged his shoulders. "It's okay… I suppose – but it's no good being like this when our friends in New York are still in danger."

"I know… but I was just saying," replied Jefferson, as Grog turned away.

The boy was a little put out by the Krogon's abrupt manner, as Meltor approached to explain the Lizardman's actions. "Take no notice of Grog… he is obviously worried about Sereny, as we all are – he's just too proud to show his emotions."

King Luccese interjected and shouted over to the Galetian. "Meltor… look – on the horizon!"

Meltor combed his fingers through his white beard and saluted his brow to shield the sun from his eyes, as he looked towards the Peronto Alps. It was an amazing sight to see Guan-yin on hoffen-back leading an army of a thousand-or-so cheering Pathylians. "That is a wonderful scene to behold, Luccese… she did it – the young Hartopian has managed to fulfill your request!"

The King cast his eyes on an even more pleasing sight and waved, as he spotted his wife riding behind Guan-yin. Vash kicked her heels and galloped ahead of the marching troops to reach her waiting husband. The Queen quickly dismounted the lively hoffen and flung her arms around Luccese's neck. "I've missed you so much… I never thought I would see you again – why have you returned so soon and what is happening on the other side of the time portal?"

Before Luccese could explain, Guan-yin arrived to welcome her King, as she also questioned his reasons. "You came back, my lord… why?"

Luccese smiled at Queen Vash and explained to both inquisitive females that the situation in New York had worsened. "I wasn't sure whether you had made it back, Guan-yin… let alone gathered the support we need - my apologies for doubting you, it would appear you have done a great job!" Explained the humble King, as he scanned the gathering army of Devonian Noblemen and Hartopians.

Meltor joined the conversation and commended the young Hartopian's efforts, as more steaming hoffen galloped towards the royal party. "And I see you have also managed to recruit my finest knights from the Galetis Empire… well done!"

"Thank you, Lord Meltor!" replied Guan-yin proudly and then called over to Grog. "Take a look at the brave warriors bringing up the rear… I think you will recognize some of them!"

The Krogon was still thinking about Sereny's plight back in New York, as the heavy sound of running koezard rumbled through the dessert ground. Grog looked up and smiled, as the giant herd of salamander-like creatures appeared from a cloud of dust led by his own faithful mount Shatar. A Krogon Warrior dismounted from the familiar white reptile and offered Grog the reigns. "Your trusted mount, my lord!"

The High Priest for Krogonia patted Shatar's neck and immediately climbed onto his back, as he leant forward to whisper. "Good to see you my old friend… will you guide me through the time portal that leads to New York help me save Sereny Ugbrooke?"

The koezard reared up in approval, as Grog winked at Jefferson. "Sorry about earlier... I am worried about our little *golden girl* and I am eager to get back and fight the Gullfather's metal monster!"

Jefferson lifted his arm to acknowledge the Krogon. "I understand... Meltor did explain!"

Guan-yin asked to speak with King Luccese and Meltor in private, as they moved away from the group. Queen Vash knew what the young High Priestess was about to say and afforded her husband a concerned look.

The King reciprocated by holding out his arm to welcome his wife and she ran over to join them. "What is it Vash?"

"Guan-yin will tell you, my darling," replied the Queen. "But please don't be too hard on her... she's very upset about the situation."

"What situation?" asked Luccese.

"Talk to her and she will tell you," insisted Vash.

King Luccese was puzzled and started to become agitated. "We don't have time for this... we have to get back to help Bradley Baker and the others – what is it that you have to tell me, Guan-yin?"

The Hartopian paused before answering. "I feel ashamed to deliver this news, my lord... but it has happened again - Varuna has escaped from the tower and has recruited a band of Hartopian sympathizers that have remained loyal to the traitor!"

"Oh no... not him as well – what do we have to do to keep our enemies under lock and key!" reacted the King angrily. "First the Shade Runner eluded us and now that tyrant... how did Varuna get away?"

Before Guan-yin could explain, Meltor asked the distraught High Priestess from the Blacklands why she felt ashamed. "It is not your fault Guan-yin... our efforts were focussed on events in New York – some mistakes here in Pathylon were bound to happen."

Guan-yin answered in a disappointed tone. "I just feel ashamed that one of my own kind continues to spoil the great name of the Hartopians... we are mostly good people but Varuna and a few mindless activists continue to stain our reputation!"

Queen Vash comforted the young High Priestess. "You still have much to learn... the King and Meltor do not think that way – Varuna is simply gutter-scum and he will never change his ways."

Luccese calmed his demeanor and agreed with the Queen. "It wouldn't matter if Varuna was a dwarf from Crystal City... he'd still attempt to get his filthy claws on my crown – anyhow as I said, we don't have time to worry about him or how he escaped right now," he declared. "We'll deal with Varuna and his cronies when we get back from New York!"

The private conversation was interrupted by a lone voice that called out from the gathering troops, as a Devonian Nobleman pointed to the sky at the incoming bird.

Within minutes, more good news filtered through to reach the King, as Ploom landed nearby. "My lord... Turpol is on his way – I've just sighted hundreds of ships sailing across the Red Ocean from Rekab," reported the Klomus Hawk. "It looks like the Gatekeeper has managed to recruit hundreds of dwarves from Crystal City... there's even a few ships carrying squadrons of Black Squirrels and Wood Ogres so maybe Captain Dray and Spew are on their way to help us too!"

A few hours passed by and the ships carrying the visitors from Rekab arrived on the shores of the Unknown Land. Ploom's assumptions proved correct and King Luccese addressed the masses in front of the entrance to the swirling Vortex, as Captain Dray and Spew stood at the front.

A temporary stage had been built to elevate the King so he could address the congregation of brave volunteers. Turpol was invited to join the senior Black Squirrel and the leader of the Wood Ogres, as Luccese firstly offered the stand to Meltor.

The old Galetian stared out at the expanse of waiting faces made up of differing creeds and colours. "I feel honoured to address you all on this day... many species from different lands are here together for one cause – to assist our allies in New York and defend our lands from the threat imposed by the evil Gullfather!" he announced and turned briefly to point at the entrance to the time portal. "The threat to our world lies beyond that gateway... by transforming into bird-like creatures - a few of us have already tried to stop the Gullfather by utilizing just our Pathylian strength and agility!" He continued. "We failed and we have to try something more effective, so please remember... once inside the vortex follow the person in front of you – do not veer from the path!"

Jefferson had been very quiet up to this point and felt empowered to call out from the crowd. "What will happen to us inside the vortex, Meltor... how can a young human like me be more effective than a powerful High Priest like you?" questioned the American boy, as a group of nearby dwarves nodded in agreement with his brave inquiry. "Surely your telepathic powers alone are stronger than all of us put together?"

King Luccese stepped forward to answer. "Do not worry Jefferson, my friends and loyal subjects... special powers will be vested in you all because Meltor will guide us along the path that leads to the

Angel of the Waters – please trust me, that's all you need to know at this stage!" he explained and gestured to Grog to stand near the entrance to the time portal. The King then stepped off the platform to offer Jefferson a comforting arm. "Nothing bad is going to happen to you inside the portal if you keep to the path, I promise… now let's do what Grog suggested – let's go to New York to defeat the Gullfather and his deathly weapon!"

Jefferson smiled nervously. "Thank you for taking time to explain, your majesty… it's very much appreciated – I think I'm ready to fight!"

Luccese bid a fond farewell to his Queen and joined Grog, as Meltor and Turpol also walked over to the entrance of the time portal. The Galetian took the first step and called back to the waiting masses. "Make sure you each enter the vortex one-by-one or the pressure inside the portal will be too much… remember to follow your lead and take the correct path – it's the only way this will work!"

Meltor's closing words were overshadowed by another cloud of dust that appeared above the entrance to the vortex. Within minutes the immediate area in front of the portal was invaded by a charging heard of hoffen carrying an army of fifty-or-so Hartopian's. The leading figure wasted no time and kicked his heels, as the snorting creatures galloped past.

Meltor drew his sword and managed to cut down half a dozen of the charging rebels from the middle of the group. "There's too many of them!" he shouted.

Grog and Luccese reacted by drawing their weapons, as the familiar lead Hartopian dashed past and leapt into the entrance of the vortex. The King wielded his sword and took out a few more riders and then shouted out in frustration, as the remaining hoffen disappeared into the swirling time portal. "That was Varuna and his band of renegades… he caught us all off-guard - we have to get after him!" he ordered, as the slow process of entering the vortex in single file began.

The Gullfather
of New York

23

Vultures from the Blacklands

Back in New York, Henley and Musgrove launched themselves off the ledge at the top of the Empire State Building and flew over to meet Bradley on a nearby skyscraper. The Buzzard was out of breath and asked. "What have you seen to make you think that the Gullfather's creation can be stopped?"

Bradley pointed his wing at Liberty's raised arm again, as the torch fired intermittent laser beams into the air. "There's a chink in the statue's armour and I intend to take advantage of it!" he declared in an elusive manner. "But we are going to need more help if my plan is to succeed... there are three things that need to happen at exactly the same time – it has to be timed to perfection if Sereny and the other children inside the cages are going to survive!"

"What are you suggesting?" asked Musgrove.

Bradley collected his thoughts. "This is how we're going to stop the Gullfather's rule of terror once and for all… first we must disconnect the torch from the crown – at the same time the coin has to be removed and the power has to be isolated from the Empire State Building's antenna so all the children including Sereny can be released from the cages!"

Henley doubted the chances of Bradley's plan succeeding. "The statue will have to be lifted off the antenna and we would need an army bigger than the whole of Pathylon's five regions to *pull off* that feat of engineering – pardon the pun!"

A sudden blast prevented Bradley from defending his plan and he covered his face, as an enormous explosion shattered the windows in the surrounding buildings. The discharge was followed by a mushroom-shaped cloud that sprang up and filled the skyline above the Met Life clock tower. The Jay recovered his composure and pointed at what first appeared to be another swirling dark cloud in the distance. "It looks like the time portal in the distance has provided us with the reinforcements we need to lift the statue from the antenna!"

Henley smiled. "You're right... the magnitude of that explosion can only mean one thing – a large number of time travellers have passed through the vortex in one go!"

Musgrove butted in and hopped around in an excited manner. "Looks like King Luccese and Meltor came good... and with the helicopters providing the additional firepower – we stand a good chance of pulling this off!"

Bradley stared more closely at the flying bird-creatures moving in a deathly formation towards them. "Let's not get too excited... they don't look very friendly!"

"I'll check it out!" squawked Henley and launched his hunched frame into the air, as he flew straight towards the giant flock. The Buzzard quickly turned in midflight and soared upwards to avoid a vicious attack from one of the huge birds. He dived down to warn Bradley and Musgrove. "Get away from there… fly as fast as your wings will take you – it's a flock of vultures from the Blacklands and they are being led by Varuna!"

Musgrove called over to the fleeing Buzzard. "How do you know it's Varuna?"

Henley did not respond and continued on his way, Bradley caught site of the gruesome flock as they neared the Empire State Building. "Can you see the larger vulture at the front?"

"Can't really miss him… he's huge!" exclaimed Musgrove.

"Look at his left wing… his feathered fingers are missing and the end of his wingtip is shaped like a hook!" stated Bradley, as the Jay followed the Buzzard's lead. "That's Varuna alright!"

"Yikes!" Musgrove chirped and flew after his friend to avoid the menacing predators.

"Let's catch up with Henley!" shouted Bradley. "It looks like he's heading for the City Hall… he probably thinks this would be a good time to regroup and I'm inclined to agree with him – we're going to need Luccese and Meltor's help more than ever, now that Varuna has arrived on the scene!"

The sly vulture caught site of the fleeing birds and muttered under his breath. "Fly away Bradley Baker... flee if you must little bird - I'll just wait for your return!" he taunted. "And when I capture your blue crested wings... I'll crush them before feeding you to my hungry Hartopian assassins!"

The prominent leader of the vulture pack circled the Empire State Building and spotted a frustrated lone seagull marching back and forth inside the observatory on the 86th floor. Varuna flew down through an opening and landed inside the large viewing gallery.

The Gullfather turned to face the intruder and scolded the strange Vulture. "Who are you and what do you want here... don't you know who I am?"

"You're the one that has saved my skin and I thought I would offer you my thanks in person... I'm Varuna by the way – from Pathylon!" revealed the scavenger.

"Never heard of you!" replied the Mafia boss. "And how could I possibly have saved you?"

Varuna snarled and snapped his hooked beak, as he cricked his bare neckline. "I hear you've been creating quite a bit of anarchy in this city of yours... I like your style – right up my street!" He laughed and held his bald head out of the opening to look up at the laser beaming across the cityscape. "And thanks to your evil antics in creating that flying statue up there... all the attention from the top brass in Pathylon has been focussed on you – that gave my loyal followers in my part of the world a chance to orchestrate my escape!"

"I don't believe you have travelled all this way just to thank me!" insisted the Gullfather.

"That's true... I've also got some scores to settle with a few individuals – and that was one of them that just flew away!" replied the confident Vulture. "Bradley Baker is the eternal chosen one and he keeps returning to my world to scupper my regal intentions!" he explained. "I think I should also warn you that more help is on its way from Pathylon...

King Luccese has amassed a great army – speaking of which, he's the other one that I have a serious score to settle with!"

"Why?" asked the intrigued gull.

"Because he wears the crown that I desire... I've borne it twice before but he keeps popping up like a bad *grobite* and taking it away from me – this time I intend to destroy Luccese once and for all!" cackled Varuna.

The Gullfather joined the Vulture at the open window frame and he also looked up at the great statue. "I like you, Varuna... I'd be happy if you and your squadron of vultures join forces with my ravens and gulls – together we can defeat Bradley Baker and King Luccese!"

"Splendid," squawked Varuna and flapped his dark scruffy wings. "So what now... how can I be of service to you, Mr. Gullfather?"

"Please... call me Don Brando!" replied the great Black-Backed Gull, as he puffed on his cigar. "Now you spoke of a crown you desired... let me show you my crown – at the top of Liberty!"

Varuna stared up at the statue again. "My, my… that's a long way up - I'm looking forward to the view!"

The Gullfather laughed and stepped out onto the ledge, as he flapped his huge wings. "I believe there's someone else you'll be interested in seeing!"

"Who would that be?" asked Varuna, as both birds launched themselves off the observatory and soared upwards keeping the contour of the statue close to their underbellies to avoid the waiting helicopters.

"The Hooded Crow!" replied the Gullfather, as they reached the crown and landed on the deep window ledge. "You probably know him as the Shade Runner!"

Ethan Darke concentrated on the outline of the stranger. "I recognize that voice," he stated, as the image of the Vulture became much clearer. "Come inside, Varuna… it's good to sense your presence – what brings you to the wonderful city of New York?"

"Most likely the same reason why you are here, Ethan… well partly at least," the Vulture suggested, as he climbed through the window into the crown. "I'm here to kill King Luccese and Bradley Baker!"

The Hooded Crow stood out of his seat and hit the control desk in anger, as the laser stopped firing. The Gullfather laughed and thanked Varuna for riling the crow into finally dislodging the coin. The fuel cells began to regenerate using the power from the antenna's feed, as Ethan Darke demanded that Varuna leave Bradley Baker to him. "The eternal chosen one took my eyes... it's important that I exact my revenge!"

The Vulture's was distracted by the unconscious Golden Eagle in the cage above the control panel. "That's Sereny Ugbrooke... you have been a busy bunch of birds!" He snarled and then concentrated his attention back to Ethan Darke's angry scowl, as he approached the Hooded Crow to offer his hooked wingtip. "Let us propose a pact... you kill the boy hero and I'll dispose of Luccese – is that a deal?"

The Shade Runner calmed his anger and locked the end of his injured wing against the vulture's strong grip. "Deal!"

of New York

24

Balto the Brave

Bradley and Musgrove waited on the steps of City Hall, as Henley entered the building and made his way to the Mayor's office. The eternal chosen one deliberately held back to make sure that his friend understood the importance of keeping the details of his true identity a secret from Captain Sharp.

Musgrove offered the concerned Jay a promise. "My Uncle doesn't need to know anything about your adoption… the last thing you need is a police officer blurting out stuff in front of your Mum and Dad – or should I say your adopt…"

"That's okay, Muzzy... I don't know what to call them either – I need more time to come to terms with it all before I can face them again," explained Bradley, as he turned to head up the steps. "But they mustn't find out that I know the truth... I want to be the one to tell them – that's if I decide to at all!"

Musgrove suggested they put the matter aside for the time being and agreed that the subject would not be broached in front of Captain Sharp.

Meanwhile Varuna's flock of wild vultures were perched in strategic positions along the metal framework of the Statue of Liberty. The monument's defensive line was further enhanced with thousands of gulls and ravens covering all vulnerable parts of the structure.

The Gullfather was still inside the lofty control room at the crown discussing the next stage of his operation with the Hooded Crow and Varuna. Raith was introduced to the Vulture but he remained very quiet, as the Mafia boss detailed his cunning plan to their latest partner in crime from Pathylon

The statue's batteries were now fully charged and a constant supply of energy was fed from the antenna to maintain a constant power supply. The Gullfather squawked about his desire to control Manhattan and he proceeded to explain. "There will be no more meddling fingers on the control panel without my permission!" He warned. "The coin *will* be activated again when the time is right... but this time the torch's guidance system will be set correctly – our primary targets are the crossing points that connect to Manhattan across the Hudson and the East Rivers!"

"Why do you want to isolate Manhattan from the rest of New York?" asked Varuna.

The Gullfather cackled and responded to the Hartopian's question. "With Manhattan cut off... the Empire State Building and its power supply will be better protected from any outside influence - I will be able to control all five boroughs of the city from here!"

Varuna wondered why the King of Pathylon was planning to return. "You have obviously spooked

Luccese... what does your evil activity in New York have to do with him?"

"You have an inquisitive mind, my dear friend... but seeing as you could soon be made King of your arcane world again – I'd better explain more about Liberty's power!" replied the excited gull, as he paced back and forth along the narrow floor in front of the control panel. He lifted a small metal cover to reveal another button. "As you can see... this one is operated by a special key and I have hidden it somewhere in the city - the torch has already been programmed to fire at the *Angel of the Waters*!"

The Hooded Crow interrupted. "I have heard of the winged Angel that walks on water spoken about in Pathylon... isn't it something to do with an entrance to many strange worlds?"

"Your interpretation of the Angel is impressive, dear Ethan!" cried the Gullfather.

Varuna asked. "So where is the *so-called* Angel you speak of and what would happen if the torch fires the laser beam at it?"

Don Brando Ceeguloni sat down heavily in his control chair, as his portly frame sank into the crimson leather. "The *Angel of the Water* is another statue situated on top of an ornate fountain in Central Park... by striking the fountain – the resulting blast will enter a super-vortex beneath the Angel!"

"How would this effect Pathylon?" asked the vulture.

The Gullfather concluded. "Pathylon has the strongest link to the fountain and could be destroyed if the time portal implodes... Luccese knows that my weapon is capable of obliterating his kingdom!" he boasted. "However, one thing is guaranteed... if the fountain is wiped out by my powerful weapon – the resulting blast will close the links to many other worlds located beyond the time portal!"

The Hartopian was furious. "We have to find the key, you idiot... what's the use in me being the new King of Pathylon if I don't have a kingdom to rule?"

"Relax... calm down, Varuna," insisted the Gullfather, as he ordered the Raven to leave the crown. "I have just given an envelope to Raith... the message inside contains the clue to where the key can be found – I've made sure the riddle isn't too hard to solve."

"To whom have you sent the message?" asked the Hooded Crow. "And why are you playing games at this late stage of events?"

The Gullfather puffed on his cigar and replied. "I've addressed the envelope for the attention of Bradley Baker of course... I think a little sport always spices things up a bit!" he laughed. "Anyhow, I'm sure your pathetic little world will survive... after all, Bradley Baker is supposed to be the eternal chosen one and I'm confident he'll be able to protect Pathylon - I'm sure he's more than capable of finding the key!"

Varuna exclaimed. "You are insane... I thought I was deluded – but you make me look like a saint!"

"Not sure I like you accusing me of being insane... but I do like the thought of the Baker boy rushing around New York like a frantic treasure hunter on a wild goose chase!" squawked the Gullfather, as he stood out of his chair and headed for a doorway that led to Liberty's raised arm. "Interesting conclusion to my forty years of hard work... I'd say, Varuna – come on let's head up to the torch for a better view!"

The Hooded Crow remained in the control room and stayed quite, as he thought to himself. "What are you up to, Don Brando... what do you mean by a *wild goose chase*?" He muttered. "I think I'd better get myself prepared for the unexpected!"

The Kingfisher stared out of his office window at one of the clock faces on the Met Life Tower in the distance. The top of the building was still lit, as the early morning shade still provided a darkened hue over the city. The time was approaching seven o'clock and only four hours remained before all the time portals around the city closed for good.

A large intimidating raven appeared at the window and startled the colourful river bird, as Raith dropped an envelope onto the ledge outside. The scraggy messenger had just delivered the clue on behalf of the Gullfather.

The Kingfisher leant out and picked up the envelope, which had a logo in the top corner depicting the head of the Mafia boss. He looked at the name written on the front and read it out loud. "This has been sent by the Gullfather and it's marked for Bradley Baker's attention."

General Crade snatched the envelope from the hesitant Mayor and proceeded to open it. "This could be important information… I don't give a damn who it's addressed to!" He grunted and revealed. "There's a card inside… it looks like some kind of riddle and it mentions something about a hidden key?"

Suddenly the doors to the Mayor's office swung open, as Henley charged in followed by Bradley and Musgrove. "We have to get a message to King Luccese… Bradley believes he has found a way to disable the statue but we need more help!"

The Kingfisher retrieved the envelope from the reluctant Heron and handed it to the Buzzard. "Maybe this will change his mind… it's marked for Bradley's attention but General Crade here decided to open it – there's a riddle written inside and I think it might be a clue to the whereabouts of a key!"

Henley passed the message to Bradley. "Here… you'd better read it out to everyone - like the Kingfisher said, it may change everything."

Bradley reopened the envelope and pulled out the card, as he read the message to himself. He then declared. "It definitely looks like a clue to the location of a key… it's only one line but take a look – I may need your help to decipher the riddle," declared the Jay and placed the card on the table; *"Anchorage has the medicine but Balto's tongue holds the key for a hero to fulfill his quest!"*

Bradley scratched his feathered head and focussed on the first word. "Anchorage… that's a place in America isn't it?"

"Yes… it's somewhere in Alaska," confirmed the Mayor. "But I can't see why the Gullfather would want to send you there – it's too remote."

Henley nodded. "The Mayor's right… we don't have much time so the Gullfather is obviously playing a game – I feel he would want to see how this plays out so the location of the key must be within view of the statue's crown."

"The word tongue could refer to a language or dialect," suggested the Kingfisher. "Maybe the key is hidden inside a book in the city library… anyhow there *has* to be a reference book about *Balto* in there – so that could be a good possibility."

Bradley asked. "Why are you so sure that there will be a book about *Balto*?" And he added. "We don't even know what or who *Balto* is!"

General Crade offered an explanation and revealed his historical knowledge of the city. The Heron proceeded to tell the story of a brave dog. "*Balto* is very famous… in January 1925, Alaskan doctors feared a deadly diphtheria epidemic would spread amongst children in Alaska. Medicine to stop the outbreak existed - but doctors needed to travel nearly a thousand miles to *Anchorage* to retrieve it. "He continued to explain in precise detail. "With no trains running that far north and the only available airplane sidelined by a frozen engine… the best chance of transporting the medicine across the icy tundra was by sled dog."

"How do know all this stuff?" asked Musgrove.

The General explained that he had studied the subject at military college. "They used the story of *Balto* to inspire the students... and I agree with the Kingfisher - the fact that Anchorage is mentioned in the riddle doesn't necessarily mean that the key is hidden that far north."

Bradley picked up the card and asked the General to be more specific. "Are you suggesting the key could be in the library then?"

The Heron paused and then offered more historical facts about the brave dog. "More than 20 sled teams coordinated to make the trip through blinding snow and sub-zero temperatures... on February 1st the package was handed off to the final team, which was led by *Balto*... they covered 53 treacherous miles in just 20 hours - newspapers and radio around the world followed the trek, fascinated by the brave team whose efforts eventually helped end the epidemic." General Crade continued his amazing story, as everyone listened intently. "*Balto* became a national hero... just 10 months after the successful mission, a sculpture was dedicated to the dog in Central Park."

"Did you say a sculpture?" asked Bradley.

"Yes," replied the General. "The sculpture depicts *Balto* surveying the distance, with his hind legs braced and a sled harness hanging from his back."

Bradley congratulated the knowledgeable Heron and hopped towards the door. "That was a good suggestion of yours, Mr. Kingfisher... but I don't believe that the key is in the library – if the Gullfather is playing a game then he would not be able to see us searching indoors from his viewpoint in the statue!" He surmised. "I believe the General has hit on something more tangible... the facts in his story certainly match the details of the riddle - we definitely need to get to Central Park!"

Musgrove chirped. "So are you suggesting that the dog may be the source of the clue... the *Balto* sculpture could be hiding the key?"

"Absolutely!" exclaimed Bradley. "Let's go!"

The Gullfather
of New York

25

Tears of the Angel

The Gullfather and Varuna had now made their way up Liberty's raised arm to the torch and they took it in turns to view the surrounding cityscape through a fixed telescope. Don Brando Ceeguloni watched with interest, as the eternal chosen one flew above the streets of Manhattan in the direction of Central Park. "I see the Jay is on his way to find the key… and he has a couple of helpers flying with him!"

Varuna took control of the telescope and spied at the three birds. "Ah, yes… the Buzzard is Henley Baker and the Robin is Musgrove Chilcott – he's the one that killed his own father by mistake!"

"Interesting… I'm intrigued to know more - who was the *Robin's* father?" inquired the Gullfather.

"The Shadow Druid!" replied Varuna.

Don Brando Ceeguloni chewed on his cigar. "Even more interesting… this is turning into quite a show – I'm going to enjoy seeing the look on all their faces when their heroic efforts prove futile in the end!"

Meanwhile King Luccese followed Meltor's lead along the twisting vortex until they reached a junction in the time portal. The army of a thousand-or-so volunteers travelled behind, whilst maintaining their single file formation.

The Galetian High Priest pointed to a gateway with strips of shining material hanging down like droplets of rain. "That's the entrance we have to take… I just hope Varuna headed in the opposite direction!"

"Where will this lead us?" asked Luccese. "And what is the entrance made from?"

"The gateway will lead us to the *Angel of the Waters*… the hanging droplets are supposed to simulate the Angel's tears and when we all pass through we should receive a pair of heavenly wings – here goes!" cried Meltor, as he entered the gateway.

A continuous series of flashing lights burst out of the entrance, as each of the King's followers passed through the draping material to receive their means of flight into the next world.

The lens of the Gullfather's telescope followed Bradley Baker, as he flew down into Central Park. The exhausted Jay landed on a terraced structure made of stone and he stared through the balustrades across the open area to view a magnificent fountain.

Henley and Musgrove landed next to Bradley and they watched in amazement, as the water flowing from the fountain's blue basin began to lift high into the air. The bronze Angel at the centre of the inverted waterfall appeared to be walking on water and a sudden blast of bright light shot up to engulf the heavenly figure.

"What's happening?" asked Musgrove.

Bradley noticed the cascading curtain of water around the edge of the basin open to reveal a swirling entrance to a time portal. "Look its Meltor... but he hasn't changed into a Kestrel – his appearance is still a Galetian but look at his back!"

Henley declared. "It works... it actually works!"

"I'm confused... what works?" asked Musgrove.

"The tears of the Angel!" exclaimed Henley. "It's a gateway inside the vortex from the Unknown Land... when we arrived in New York from Pathylon before – we chose the path that led to the Met Life Tower!" he explained and brushed his plumage. "It's the safest and most direct route, but as you can see... it has the side effects of transforming you into a bird!"

Bradley was amazed as King Luccese and Grog exited the fountain. "So you get to keep your original form but still grow wings?"

Henley nodded. "Yes... the wings of an Angel but I think the Gullfather has set a trap!"

"What do you mean?" asked Bradley.

"I believe that the fountain has always been his main target and if we don't find that key it will be destroyed!" replied Henley, as he took to the air again. "Let's find the Balto sculpture... your destiny depends on it!"

Bradley suggested Musgrove go and welcome King Luccese. "Tell him where me and Henley are going and what the Gullfather is up to!" he ordered and took flight to join the Buzzard.

Henley soon spotted another clearing in the park. "There he is!" he declared, as the statue of a dog appeared between some trees.

Bradley caught up with the Buzzard before he had chance to land and asked. "What did you mean back there... my destiny depends on it?"

Henley paused before delivering some very important news relating to Bradley's true identity. "Another world lies beyond the fountain... if the laser beam from the Gullfather's weapon destroys the time portal – you will never get to meet your real mother!"

The two birds landed next to the sculpture of Balto, as Bradley gasped for breath. The shock of hearing that his birth mother could still be alive had caused a great pain in his chest.

Henley tried to comfort his son but the quivering Jay pushed him aside and moved to the head of the sculpture. Bradley looked at the Buzzard and declared. "I assumed my real Mother was dead... otherwise why give me away – I feel worthless!"

"It wasn't like that, Bradley... that's not what happened," said Henley. "When you were born your Mother and I were very happy... you were still a small baby when they took her away!"

"Who took her away and where did all this happen?" asked Bradley in a confused manner.

Henley tried to explain. "Your Mother ruled over a land called Aakoria... I was made King when I married her because she held the status of Queen – she had many enemies just like Luccese has in Pathylon," he explained. "A female rival called Grendal was jealous of my marriage to your Mother and she kidnapped her... your Mother was taken to a mountainous prison at the far reaches Aakoria and I never saw her again."

Bradley's demeanor changed and he asked in a caring tone. "What was my real Mother's name?"

"Her name *is* Talitha and I still believe she is alive... someday, I will return to Aakoria to find her – I promise!" Henley smiled and thought back, as an image of his beautiful Queen's face filled his mind. "You look a bit like your Mother... she was a good person and she would never have given you up if she had been given the choice."

"What does she look like?" asked Bradley.

Henley still had his Queen's face clearly in his mind. "Aakorians are renowned for their beauty... they are very much like humans, which is why you appear normal when you are in your own world – not like now of course," he laughed. "Although you do make an excellent Jay with your striking blue feathers and all!"

Bradley grinned. "But you are a Devonian... you have horns – will I grow horns too?"

"That I don't know... if you do grow horns – they won't start to show until you are at least thirteen years old," confirmed the Buzzard, as he watched Bradley move towards Balto's head.

"So how did I end up living in Yorkshire with my parents?" asked Bradley, as he placed his feathered hand inside the mouth of the bronze statue.

"That's a long story... when Grendal's evil henchmen took your Mother, I tried desperately to find her but it's as though she had disappeared from the face of Aakoria – the thought did cross my mind that she had been killed," explained the tearful Buzzard. "I couldn't bear to rule the kingdom without Talitha so I left and took you with me back to Pathylon... to my homeland of Devonia and that's where I met Meltor – the High Priest arranged our transportation to the outside world and that's when I met Patrick Baker via an adoption agency and they agreed to bring you up as their own!"

"Do my parents in Sandmouth know I am your Son.... and how come your surname is Baker if you're not actually related to my adopted father?" asked Bradley has he fumbled inside the dog's mouth to retrieve the hidden key beneath its tongue.

"No... they just think I was fostering you on behalf of social services... Patrick felt it was important for me to stay in touch and sort of accepted me as his brother - I ended up living with your adoptive parents for a while before my accident in the mine," explained Henley. "And I know what you're thinking... you weren't even born when I had my accident!"

"You read my mind," replied Bradley, as he finally located the key under Balto's tongue. "Eureka... I got it!"

"Well done!" cried Henley and concluded the conversation. "Well that's the strange thing about time travel... weird things happen – now let's get that key back to the others and I'll try to explain it some other time!"

The Gullfather's telescope lens was still fixed firmly on the scene around the sculpture and the huge gull squawked loudly, as the dog began to transform. "That's impossible... my plan is back firing – that wasn't supposed to happen!" he cried, as the outer coat of the bronze statue began to disintegrate to reveal a real dog beneath.

Bradley pulled his wing tip out of the canine's mouth and stumbled back, as the statue of Balto transformed into a familiar friend. "Hello Master, barked the Burnese Mountain Dog... not sure the feathered look suits you!" He teased and proceeded to lick the Jay's face.

"It's great to see you old boy!" cawed Bradley and then looked over to Henley. "Come on, Father... we've got the key so let's head back to the fountain!"

The Buzzard opened his wings and launched his magnificent frame into the air, as K3 looked totally confused. "That's Henley... he's supposed to be your Uncle but you've just called him Father?"

Bradley patted his trusted pet on the back and then flew into the air to join Henley. "It's a very long story... I'll tell you all about it later but first we've got to get this key up to the crown of Liberty before that torch destroys my only chance of seeing my real mother again - that's if she's still alive!"

"I'll take your word on that!" barked K3, as the confused hound shrugged off the sled harness and bound across the park in pursuit of the two birds.

26

The Battle for New York

The Gullfather remained in the torch with Varuna and traversed the telescope to view one of the clock faces that adorned the Met Life Tower. The minute hand moved slowly onto the six to indicate thirty minutes passed ten. That meant there was only half an hour to go before the entrances to the time portals in the city would close automatically and then the allies would be trapped in New York.

Don Brando Ceeguloni sniggered, as he angled the telescope back across the cityscape and focussed the lens to view the fountain in Central Park. The immediate area around the *Angel of the Waters* was now filled with battalions of winged creatures from Pathylon and Rekab.

The Gullfather zoomed in to watch Bradley Baker welcome a young human, as Jefferson tipped his baseball cap. Don Brando squawked quietly to himself, as he moved the telescope to track and observe the two friends rejoin the rest of the main group. "The eternal chosen is now talking to King Luccese... they must be discussing their plans for an attack on the Statue of Liberty," assumed the Mafia boss, as he zoomed in further to focus on the end of the Jay's wingtip and uttered his concerns to Varuna. "Looks like the boy hero still has the key... I've no doubt that Luccese and his army of angel-winged vigilantes will be launching an assault any minute – we need to warn the Hooded Crow inside the crown!"

The cigar-smoking gangster was correct in his assumption and the attack began sooner than expected, as the helicopter gunships reappeared around the statue. General Crane had given Captain Sharp the order to prepare for a full military onslaught, as a pelican pilot hovered above the torch.

The Gullfather and the Hartopian were now trapped inside the torch's viewing gallery, as the incensed vulture screeched. "Now what do we do?" squawked Varuna. "If we try to fly out of here, those machines will shoot us down.

"Stop complaining... I'll make a quick call – the Hooded Crow is more than capable of looking after things!" replied the arrogant mobster, as he picked up a handheld communication unit and spoke with Ethan Darke in the crown below. "The allies still seem reluctant to fire at the statue while the children are secured inside their cages... we have no option but to stay in the torch, the penguins will protect us as long as they remain in their cages – we have to be patient and wait until the torch has destroyed the fountain but you must ensure the coin remains in the control panel!"

The Hooded Crow returned an affirmative response. "Don't worry, Don Brando... I'll look after things from here – the coin is safe!" he cawed and looked up at the cage that secured Sereny. "The golden girl is still sleeping... so her brain will be ready to trigger the firing mechanism of the laser when needed – in the meantime, shall I start destroying the bridges that span the East River?"

"Excellent... and yes – take out the Brooklyn Bridge for starters!" squawked the Gullfather, as the torch maneuvered to the left. "The fate of Manhattan is now in your capable hands!" he affirmed, as the laser fired to obliterate the iconic bridge. The contented gull disconnected the receiver and turned to face Varuna. "Let that be proof of my weapon's power to the Kingfisher and his new friends!"

Meanwhile inside the Mayor's office, General Crade and the Kingfisher were in constant communication with the leaders from Pathylon and Rekab. The television screened the images of devastation around Brooklyn Bridge, as news channels across the city maintained their live coverage of events.

Captain Sharp had already left City Hall and he flew over Central Park to act as liaison between the Army and Luccese's forces. The pigeon police officer arrived at base camp in time to witness the angel-winged battalions make their final preparations for action. He approached the Pathylian King. "Your Majesty... it may be wise for you to converse with your senior leaders in private – I have just flown via the Statue of Liberty and it looks like the Gullfather is monitoring your movements with a telescope from the torch!" He suggested. "Varuna is with him and they are hemmed in by Crade's helicopters... we've just lost the Brooklyn Bridge and Ethan Darke appears to be controlling the laser from inside the crown!"

Luccese nodded. "Thank you, Captain Sharp... I'll arrange for my battle planning team to meet me over there!" He replied and pointed to the terrace across from the fountain. "Meltor... please gather the leaders together and join me beneath the arches!"

"Yes, my lord!" retorted the Galetian High Priest and delivered the King's instruction to the others.

It did not take long for everyone to gather beneath the terrace, safely away from the Gullfather's prying eyes. Henley was called over and Bradley, Musgrove, Jefferson and K3 joined him to hear the King's secret address. Luccese stood on a raised step to instruct the group of dignitaries in relation to their individual tasks. "Dear friends and allies... this is probably the most important mission we will ever have to undertake – it feels strange to prepare for a battle so far away from our own lands, but our future depends on the destruction of the laser inside that giant torch," he reiterated. "The mission is dangerous and I have already spoken with the eternal chosen one... so here's what I want each of you to do!"

Bradley felt proud to have been consulted and stroked K3's neck, as he stood aside with Musgrove. "The adrenalin is starting to kick in, Muzzy... this adventure is about to reach an amazing climax!" he declared and looked over to his friend's uncle.

Captain Sharp's stance was rigid, as he puffed out his chest and listened to his part of the brief. It would be the pigeon's responsibility to ensure that General Crade's helicopter gunships hit their intended target. Luccese looked over to the police officer and explained his role. "Bradley informs me there is a chink in the statue's armour... the elbow of Liberty's raised arm is weak - I'm relying on you to hit it hard when the time is right!"

"I'll liaise with General Crade on the matter, sir!" replied the attentive pigeon, as he removed his peaked blue cap and saluted the King. "The N.Y.P.P.D is at your service, your majesty!"

Luccese smiled at the enthusiastic pigeon and then turned to instruct the others. "Captain Dray and his legion of Black Squirrels have been told to engage with Varuna's vultures, whilst Meltor and Henley will lead the Galetians and Devonians against the Gullfather's mobster gulls and ravens!" he declared. "Grog and Spew... I'd like you to unite the Krogon Warriors and the Wood Ogres and detach Liberty from the antenna!"

Grog winked at the giant Wood Ogre and affirmed the King's request. "No problem, sire!"

That left Turpol and Jefferson, who were set the important task of leading the dwarves from Crystal City into the skeleton of the statue to co-ordinate the release all 364 penguin children from their cages.

Luccese deliberately omitted to mention the 365th gifted and talented child from Turpol's brief, as he turned to Musgrove. "The release of the golden girl will rest with you, Muzzy... I'm sure you will be pleased to take on the responsibility of freeing your friend from Sandmouth!"

"I'll do my best, your Majesty!" replied the nervous Robin and afforded Bradley a reassuring smile.

The King finally turned to face the Jay. "Your task is probably the most difficult of all," insisted Luccese, as he placed his strong hand on the Bradley's blue-feathered shoulders. "Your role as the eternal chosen one is yet again called into action, my brave friend... you will need to insert the key and also retrieve the sacred grobite from the crown - your actions alone will not only save Manhattan but will also secure the time portal that leads to your Mother's world!"

Bradley was shocked to hear the King speak of his personal secret. "How did you know about my real Mother and her whereabouts?"

The King held the emotional Jay affront in a reassuring embrace. "We have always known... and each member of the Pathylian Royal Congress swore an oath to guard your true identity at any cost – don't forget that you are the protector of our world!"

"I fully understand your reason for guarding my true identity... it's just that I'm still a bit shocked about the whole thing," explained Bradley. "But don't worry, your Majesty... I won't let you down!" he promised and stepped back to shake the King's royal hand. "I am proud to be the eternal chosen one and I will do all I can to continue in my quest to protect the arcane world of Pathylon!"

Luccese replied in a confident tone. "Of that I have no doubt... but please be aware of Ethan Darke – he will be waiting to repay you for your actions!"

Musgrove also admired his friend's brave words and called over to the King. "What about the Gullfather and Varuna in the torch?"

Luccese smiled. "Leave those two evil specimens to me!" He promised and then shouted across to his squadron leaders. "Make sure your people are reminded that all the time portals will close when our allotted time in this world runs out... remember, if any of the hands on the clock towers strike eleven – those left behind will be unable to return home to their loved ones!"

The battle for New York had officially begun and Meltor ordered sentries to be posted at the entrance of each time portal to ensure a rapid exit should the allies run out of time. Captain Sharp flew ahead to liaise with the helicopter gunships, while Grog and Spew gathered their Krogon Warriors and Wood Ogres together. Turpol and Jefferson led the dwarves, as they launched their short frames off the ground followed by Captain Dray and the squadron of Black Squirrels.

Luccese held back and watched with pride, as his army of winged regiments filled the Manhattan skyline. Meltor spread his wings and bid his King good luck, as the High Priest took to the air with his battalion of angel-winged Galetians.

Henley offered Bradley some final words of comfort, as they prepared to join the mission. "I know the discovery of your true identity has come as a massive shock… now put it to the back of your mind and try to keep your focus – you must prevent the laser weapon from firing at the fountain." He stated and knelt down in front of his son. "If for whatever reason you fail to isolate the torch… just make sure you retrieve the coin – then at least the chances of meeting your real Mother may still be possible."

Musgrove pulled on the Jay's wing and urged him to take flight. "We have to go, Bradley."

"Yes… I coming, Muzzy," replied Bradley and cast a hopeful glance at Henley, as a large group of Devonians gathered around. "I hope this isn't our final goodbye, Father!"

Luccese flew down and interrupted the emotional encounter, as the King's broad wingspan cast an impressive golden glow over the birds. He insisted they both take to the sky. "Come on… the battle for New York has started – the time for talking is over!"

Musgrove hovered overhead and chirped a friendly call, as the Robin swooped and tipped his wing. "Good luck, Brad… see you up at the crown!"

27

Trapped in the Torch

The battle intensified and reached a heightened level of activity, as the allies fought fiercely with the Gullfather's henchmen. The fatal squawking sound of injured birds filled the air, as the relentless fighting ensued. The stationary vehicles in the streets below were littered with a tirade of fallen carcasses, as feathered bodies crashed down like heavy rain.

The city's pigeon police tried to instill some kind of order on the streets below and a sparrow climbed out of his yellow cab. The taxi driver scraped a dead tern from his bloodstained windscreen and called out to an officer. "This is like Armageddon… its total chaos up there!"

The uniformed pigeon offered some words of reassurance to the sparrow. "Try not to panic… the Kingfisher is working with our friends from the outside worlds - just pray they stop the Gullfather before the whole city is covered in blood!"

High above the skyscrapers, Varuna's Hartopian vultures were quickly overpowered by Captain Dray and his agile Black Squirrels. Whilst Meltor and Henley led their united battalions to a glorious victory against the evil flocks of seagulls, ravens and terns.

Raith escaped the deathly onslaught to seek sanctuary back inside the crown, as the Hooded Crow tried desperately to retain control. "The flying Wood Ogres and Krogons have managed to detach Liberty from the antenna!" he cawed, as the statue began to rise into the air. The Raven tried to activate the mechanical wings but the power feed from the Empire State Building was no longer available.

King Luccese focussed his attention on the torch and avoided the misfiring laser beam, as he landed safely on top of the metal shaped flame. He leant over and forced his muscular arm through the window and grabbed hold of the squealing Vulture. "Come here you weasel… we have some unfinished business to take care of!" He threatened and wrapped his muscular biceps around the Vulture's neck. Varuna was pulled clear of the viewing gallery, as the vengeful King shouted. "This time I will not allow you to escape… this is where it ends for you!" he bellowed and rendered the evil bird's wings useless.

Varuna squawked a defiant cry, as he felt the bones crack beneath his feathers. "I hope you and your crown will be very happy together – looks like neither of us will ever get to rule Pathylon again!" he boasted, as his eyes viewed the clock face on the Met Life Tower. "You're running out of time, Luccese!" he screamed, as the King released his hold to allow the Hartopian to fall to his death.

The Gullfather followed the trajectory of the Hartopian's *death fall*, as Varuna's screaming flightless shape passed the busy Krogons and Wood Ogres before crashing into the Hudson.

Luccese took some time to catch his breath and hovered majestically over the torch, as he called over to Captain Sharp. "Make sure you keep in regular contact with Crade in the Mayor's office... the General must maintain the helicopter gunship's positions around the torch to prevent the Gullfather from escaping!"

"Yes... your Majesty – I'll radio the General now!" replied the police officer.

Luccese flew down to join Grog and Spew at the feet of Liberty, as he helped the Krogons and Tree Ogres to carry the heavy skeletal frame back towards Liberty Island. The King looked up and called out, as he spotted the *eternal chosen one* flying towards the crown. "Retrieve the coin and use the power bestowed upon you to save our worlds!"

Bradley Baker acknowledged Luccese by dipping his wings to enter the crown, as he confronted the Hooded Crow and they wrestled at the controls.

Musgrove arrived to support his friend and sneaked up behind Raith, as he rendered the Raven unconscious. The agile Robin then climbed on the top

316

of the control panel and reached up to unfasten the straps that secured Sereny inside the cage. "Wow... you've changed into an eagle – when did that happen?"

"I can't remember much about it... although I do recall dreaming about my new wings lifting this statue into the air!" she replied and then recognised the familiar blue colours of a bird struggling to overpower Ethan Darke. "Bradley... be careful!" She shouted, as the Shade Runner picked up a broken piece of chair and crashed the blunt metal object across the Jay's beak.

"Arrrrrgghhhh!" cawed Bradley, as he fell backwards.

Musgrove jumped down to help his friend and Sereny climbed out of her cage to assist. They both dived on top of the startled crow and dislocated one of his shoulders. Sereny pinned him to the floor, as the brave Robin reached out for a length of electrical cable and tied the Shade Runner's damaged wing behind his back.

Bradley recovered his composure then rubbed his head and checked to ensure his beak was still intact, as Raith opened his eyes. The Raven quickly grabbed the Jay's leg and pulled him across the floor. "Get over here, Baker boy... you've caused enough trouble!"

Sereny turned to see Raith's wing wrapped around Bradley's neck, as she left Musgrove to restrain the Hooded Crow. "Bradley's in trouble... he needs help!" she exclaimed and revealed her huge eagle talons, as she leapt on top of the Raven's back.

"What the....!" cawed Raith, as Sereny's sharp claws penetrated deep into his flesh. "Arrrrrgghhhh!" he screeched and released his grip.

Bradley reacted by landing a knock-out blow to bird's beak and Raith crumpled to the floor, as the Jay kicked the limp bird from his legs. "Thanks, Sereny... I owe you one – loving the new look, by the way!"

"No problem, Bradley... any time!" smiled the young eagle, as the statue shuddered violently and a loud thud echoed through the structure. "What was that?"

Bradley moved over to help Musgrove, who was struggling to restrain the Hooded Crow and offered Sereny a possible reason for the sudden jolt to the statue. "I think Liberty has just been struck by one of the missiles from the helicopters!" he exclaimed and moved over to look out of the viewing gallery to witness the statue's raised arm broken at the elbow. "Yes... I was right – one of the missiles from the helicopter gunships has managed to hit the piece of shrapnel I told them about!"

Musgrove recalled his father's account of the 1916 disaster. "You mean after all this time... a piece of stray metal from the *Black Tom* explosion has helped to defeat the Gullfather's weapon – now that's what I call a serious case of a plan *seriously* back firing!"

"It sure looks that way!" exclaimed Bradley.

Sereny hooked her head out of the open window frame and stared up at the swinging torch which was crashing against the upper part of the arm. "The plan has back fired, alright... the weapon has been destroyed and the Gullfather is trapped inside the torch – New York is safe at last!"

"Not quite!" replied Bradley, as he pulled the key from his pocket. "I still need to isolate the laser from the batteries... the fountain in Central park is still vulnerable!" He declared, as he lifted the cover on the control panel. "But before I insert the key... I need to retrieve this little baby first!" he insisted and prized the coin out of the desk, as the grobite vibrated.

At that moment the straps securing all the juvenile penguins released, as Jefferson and Turpol's team of dwarves seized their opportunity to grab the gifted and talented children.

Sereny reeped. "The children are safe... Jefferson and the Gatekeeper are leading them away from the statue - it looks like they are heading across the river towards the time portal in the New Jersey Journal building!" She screamed in an exited tone and turned to congratulate the Jay, as the crown suddenly filled with green smoke. "Where did Bradley go?"

Musgrove closed his eyes to protect them from the thick smoke, as he felt his way over to join Sereny.

The emerald cloud began to disperse, as the two birds quickly realized that their friend had disappeared and the Robin shouted. "Where did he go?"

There was an eerie silence and then a familiar voice delivered a calm retort. "I'm over here!" replied the boy as he stepped through the clearing smoke.

"Bradley... you've changed back to normal – you're a boy again!" exclaimed Sereny. "It must be the sacred grobite's magic working again... just like it did when Jefferson had the coin!"

The fledgling eagle was right, the coin had transformed Bradley back into his human form. The sacred grobite was now firmly secured in his clenched fist, as he held out the key and inserted it into the top of the button. "Here goes!" he exclaimed.

Ethan Darke was enraged to see his nemesis return to human form, as he struggled to release the cable that strapped his wings. The Shade Runner kicked out, as he lay on the floor and called out his warning. "Don't turn the key... the Gullfather has led you on a *wild goose chase* – he has tricked us all!"

Bradley ignored the tethered crow and inserted the key to activate the button, as Liberty shook violently. The helpless Mafia boss was still trapped inside the torch, as the battery indicator on the control panel began to flash and the twisted metal arm swung like a pendulum at the point where the missile had hit the shrapnel. The boy hero held firmly onto the coin, as the last drop of energy from the fuel cells fed into the weapon's firing mechanism. "That's impossible... the key should have isolated the power to the torch!"

A piece of heavy paneling fell down and crushed the crow's leg, as the statue leaned slightly. Ethan Darke cried out as the weight of the unit snapped his lower limb. "Arrrrrgghhhh... we're all doomed!"

Bradley sensed an immediate danger and insisted that Musgrove and Sereny fly away to a safe distance. "Get out of here you two... this things going to crumble – there's no point in us all being killed!"

Sereny rushed over to Bradley and wrapped her wings around his body. "I'll carry you!" she insisted and attempted to lift. "Arrrrrgghhhh... it's no good you're too heavy – Muzzy get over here and help!"

Musgrove tried to assist but the boy's human frame was still too weighty for both young birds to lift, as Bradley afforded his two friends an appreciative look. "Thanks for trying guys... now go – you have to get off the statue before it's destroyed!"

Sereny began to weep, as Musgrove pulled her away. "Bradley's right... we have to go!"

"No... we can get more help!" insisted the distraught Golden Eagle and rushed over to the viewing gallery. "Surely some of the other birds can help us!" She reeped and looked out to witness the allied forces retreating. "I don't believe it... they're fleeing – they're abandoning us!"

Bradley stepped over to console Sereny. "They're not abandoning us... look at the clock face on the Met Life Tower – the minute hand is about strike eleven o'clock," he explained calmly. "Now you two need to get to the Jersey City portal or you'll be stuck in this time dimension forever... please go – I've got the coin back so there could be a chance I can still isolate the laser," he insisted and stroked the eagle's sad face. "Let me take it from here!"

Sereny grabbed Bradley again and whispered in his ear. "I love you, Bradley Baker."

"I know… now get out of here," replied the boy, as Sereny joined Musgrove on the ledge. They reluctantly launched themselves away from the crown and flew in the direction of the Jersey Journal clock tower, as a fearful tear rolled down Bradley's cheek. The boy turned his attention to his final task and stared over at the key sticking out from the button on the control panel, as he muttered out loud. "Let's hope that thing has worked… although, I've got a feeling Ethan is right - the Gullfather may still have the last laugh!"

The boy's quiet outburst was overheard by the Hooded Crow, as he nursed his wounded leg and cawed to confirm Bradley's worst fears. "Did you not think that solving the clue was just a little too simple… the Gullfather knew you would find the key easily because he wanted you to activate the laser - not deactivate it!"

"Oh no… the time portal at the fountain – it will be obliterated!" exclaimed the boy, as he stood and looked out of the crown towards Central Park. "The entrance to Aakoria will be destroyed and I'll never see my real mother again... what have I done?"

Within seconds the torch began to glow, as a spark of electricity arced across the damaged elbow joint of Liberty's arm. A blinding beam of energy flashed across the Manhattan skyline, as the weapon's cruel strike hit the basin below the fountain.

The Gullfather had achieved his goal, as the elbow joint finally gave way. The lower arm and the attached torch began its perilous journey into the Hudson below, as the laser stopped emitting its beam of terror. The stricken Mafia boss crawled over to the edge of the falling viewing gallery and Don Brando Ceeguloni stared up towards the crown of Liberty. He removed the smoking cigar from his beak and called out to the defeated boy, as Bradley looked down to witness the laughing seagull. The Gullfather squawked his final taunt. "You lost Bradley Baker.... ha'ha'ha'ha'-ha – and I won!"

CRASSHHHHHHHH!!!!! SPLASSSHHHHH!!!!
The torch hit the water hard and exploded on impact,

as a ball of fire shot into the air. The burning remains of the metal torch sank and a cloud of falling feathers landed softly on the surface of the water next to a floating cigar.

The Statue of Liberty continued to shake, as Bradley focussed his attention on a much more powerful explosion in Central Park. A white light spread out from the damaged fountain in a circular formation and the resulting energy-wave cleared everything in its path, as the blast continued on its devastating journey towards Liberty Island.

Bradley shielded his eyes, as the impact of the discharge howled through the open frames of the crown's windows and swept him off his feet. The strong gust tossed his body against the control panel and he struck his head on a metal lever. The boy was rendered unconscious and his eyes stayed wide open, as he slumped to the floor. The sacred grobite remained secure in his clenched fist and the coin started to vibrate, as the wind continued to howl around his ears and his eyelids finally closed.

28

The Queen of Australia!

Nearly six months had passed since the multiple explosions devastated the famous landmarks of New York City. A little girl walked hand-in-hand with her mother down a familiar corridor inside the hospital on 5th Avenue. Frannie Baker had a brightly wrapped gift tucked neatly under her other arm, as she looked up at her mother with a very excited expression.

Margaret and her five year old daughter continued along the corridor until they arrived at the entrance to a private ward. They entered the room and walked quietly towards the bed where a boy lay very still with bandages wrapped around his forehead. A network of cables hung from contact points on the boy's body, as the monitoring units either side bleeped intermittently. Frannie whispered to her mother and climbed up onto the bed, as her older brother's eyelids flickered. "Is Bradley still in a coma?"

"Sort of... he's been drifting in and out but hopefully he'll wake up soon – now give me the present and I'll put it with the others," replied Margaret, as her inquisitive daughter began to fidget on the edge of the bed.

Frannie poked her nose then scratched the cheek of her bottom and asked. "Do you think he will call things out in his sleep again today, Mummy?"

"Most probably, my dear... he's been doing a lot of that over the past few weeks – anyhow, the consultant said it was a good sign and he should be fully awake soon," declared Margaret. "Not sure what he was slurring about yesterday, though... he kept asking about the *Queen of Australia* or something like that – he must have been dreaming about one of his *make-believe* adventures again!"

"Can I open his card?" asked Frannie, as an attractive female doctor entered the room closely followed by a nurse. The cheeky little red-head smiled at the two medics, as the nurse administered Bradley's painkillers. "It was my brother's birthday yesterday... he's a teenager now!"

Margaret agreed to let Frannie open the card, as the uneasy doctor adjusted her dark-rimmed spectacles and afforded the girl a nervous smile. The nurse checked Bradley's blood pressure, as his concerned mother took the card and stood it next to the gift. "I can't believe my boy is thirteen years old... I just hope he comes back to us in time to celebrate his birthday properly – the whole ordeal has been so tragic."

The nurse completed her check-up and the doctor smiled again politely, as Frannie looked at the name badge on her uniform. "You don't say much for an important person, do you... errrr – Dr. Zoe Sparrow!"

Margaret apologized for her daughter's frankness. "I'm sorry, doctor... Frannie is just excited about her brother's progress – the nice consultant we saw yesterday said he could wake from the coma at any moment."

Dr. Sparrow broke her silence and confirmed the boy's improved condition, as she delivered a fictitious retort. "I'm so sorry you have had to endure so much uncertainty over the last few months... your Son was very lucky to survive the terrorist attacks on New York."

"I know... we are all just so glad he is alive," replied Margaret and then seized the opportunity to talk about the recent atrocities. "It's not the same without the Brooklyn Bridge... and what about the Statue of Liberty – it's disgusting what those nasty people did to your wonderful city!"

"Errrrr... yes – well, ermmmm!" replied the doctor and tried to avoid commenting any further, as she stepped back to allow her colleague to move around the bed.

The nurse felt uncomfortable with the hastened silence and felt obliged to ask the pleasant lady how she had been coping over the past six months. "You're a long way from home... it must have come as quite a shock – with your Son being so far away from you when all this happened?"

"Yes, I didn't expect to be flying out to New York to visit my Son under such extreme conditions... he came over here during the Easter holiday to stay with his friend Jefferson - it's the first time we had allowed him to fly without us and look what happened!" explained Margaret, as she wiped away a few tears. "My husband had to fly back to England last week to make sure our hotel business was still in one piece... we left it in the capable hands of my sister Vera - heaven knows what state the rooms are in!" she sighed. "Frannie and I have been staying with the Crabtree's in Hudson Valley, whilst Bradley has been recovering in your lovely hospital."

Frannie comforted her mother. "Don't cry Mum... everything will be okay!" she insisted and held her brother's hand. "Come on Bradley... wake up – I've got you a lovely birthday present!"

Bradley's eyelids flickered again and Margaret screamed. "He's coming round... my *Son* is waking up!"

The nurse pressed a button on the wall and the door of the room burst open, as more medical staff entered to aid the patient's recovery. They were followed by another familiar individual and Dr. Sparrow welcomed the African American boy, as she whispered in his ear. "Good to see you again, Jefferson... he's just waking up – we need to make sure he doesn't say anything untoward to his *Mother*."

"Great to see your wings *or should I say your arms* have fully recovered, Flaglan... now can you come up with an excuse to get Margaret and Frannie out of the room?" insisted Jefferson. "So I can explain everything to Bradley before he *spills the beans*."

"Leave it to me," replied Flaglan, as she moved over to the bed and spoke with Margaret. "I'm afraid I'll have to ask you both to step outside until Bradley has fully regained consciousness... seeing you and his little sister may come as a bit of a shock – he's not aware of anything that's happened over the past six months so I'm sure you'll understand that he will need to be brought back into reality very gently."

Margaret looked displeased at the *fake* doctor's suggestion but understood her concerns. Her disappointment was averted when she noticed Jefferson standing at the back of the room. "Oh, hello... I didn't hear you come in – it looks like Bradley is about to wake up!"

Jefferson approached Margaret to comfort her and put his arms around her shoulders, as Flaglan repeated her request. "I'm sorry, Mrs. Baker but I think it would be best if you leave now... I'll call you back in as soon as I feel Bradley is ready to speak with you – if you like, Jefferson could stay to offer some friendly support!"

Margaret smiled at Jefferson. "I think Bradley would like that... would you mind staying here?"

The boy nodded. "Of course, Mrs. Baker."

Flaglan offered Jefferson a look of disbelief, as Margaret and Frannie reluctantly left the room. "Well that worked out okay... now, let's see what Bradley has to say!"

The eternal chosen one opened his eyes and struggled to focus his blurred vision on the group of faces looking down, as the white lights above their heads formed a bright halo. "Where am I?" He asked.

A familiar voice replied. "You're in a hospital… in New York."

"Is that you, Jefferson?" asked Bradley.

Jefferson nodded and held his friend's hand. "Yep, it's me buddy… you've just woken up – you've been in a coma for about six months!"

"I take it I survived the explosion then?" slurred Bradley, as the weary boy recalled the last few moments before he passed out. "I don't understand why we're all still in New York?" he muttered, as he lifted his hand to feel the bandages around his head. "The blast from the fountain must have wiped out most of the city… including this hospital - so how come Manhattan survived?"

Flaglan noticed the puzzled looks on the faces of the attentive medics, as the nurse began to query the patient's unusual outbursts. To avoid any more probing questions, the masquerading doctor instructed them all to leave the room immediately and they reluctantly heeded her request.

As the staff left the room, Bradley recognised Flaglan's voice. "Glad you're feeling better... have your wings fully healed yet?" asked the confused boy, as his vision became much clearer. "Hang on... you've change back – where have your feathers gone?"

Jefferson interrupted. "You're not in the New York City you think you're in... you're back in your own world – everyone managed to reach their respective time portals before the clocks struck eleven!"

Bradley looked confused. "Have I just woke up from a really bad dream... where are Musgrove and Sereny - did they get away okay and what about the penguins and why is Flaglan here?"

"No and yes... so many questions!" replied Jefferson. "It wasn't a dream, Bradley... both Musgrove and Sereny managed to reach the vortex beneath the Jersey Journal Building in time before it closed - everyone arrived safely back in Sandmouth, including Flaglan, the police officers and the missing school children." He confirmed. "King Luccese thought it best for Flaglan to stay in our world until she had made a full recovery and to make sure the coin was safely back in your possession!"

Bradley was especially pleased to hear that his friends had made it back to Sandmouth. He thought about the last words Sereny uttered and smiled to himself. "I'm looking forward to seeing the *golden girl* again!"

Flaglan ignored the boy's obvious infatuation with the girl and informed Bradley that Varuna had been killed. "King Luccese finally managed to eradicate the mindless moron... I still can't get over the fact that I liaised with that idiot in the past – still that's a few chapters well and truly closed."

Bradley asked about the Shade Runner. "What about Ethan Darke... did he survive?"

Flaglan shook her head. "We're not sure... you were holding the coin when we found you – that's what saved you," she explained. "As for the Hooded Crow... there was no sign of his body – so he could have escaped but I doubt he would have survived the blast."

Jefferson informed Bradley that Margaret and Frannie were waiting outside the room. "Can you remember anything about what Henley told you… do you remember having the blood transfusion and finding out about your true identity?"

Bradley paused for a moment and stared at the number *thirteen* printed on the standing card opened by Frannie, as he nodded. "Yes, I remember everything… but hang on a minute – is that *my* birthday card?"

"Yes… your thirteenth birthday was yesterday," replied Jefferson. "What significance does it have on whether you tell Margaret the truth or not?"

"Errrr… nothing," muttered Bradley, as he thought more about what Henley had told him. "I guess my adopted Mother doesn't really need to know anything… after all I'm never going to find out whether my real Mother is still alive, now that the fountain has been destroyed – it's probably best if we just carry on as if nothing happened."

Flaglan agreed and acknowledged the boy's brave decision. "Shall I ask them to come in then?"

Bradley's mind seemed to be elsewhere, as he stammered. "Errrr…yes – please do!"

Margaret and Frannie rushed into the room and their excited screams could be heard down the corridor, as a hooded figure strode slowly towards the private ward.

Bradley smiled at all the fuss his little sister was making and she handed him her present. He opened the wrapping to pull out a rather expensive looking dog collar from a *Macy's Department Store* box and it immediately reminded him of the incident with the Balto statue. "A new collar for K3… that's really nice, thank you Frannie – and how is the old fella?"

"Snoring in his basket back home I expect!" replied Frannie, as she hugged her older brother. "So glad you have woken up in time for your birthday!"

Margaret continued to converse in an enthusiastic manner but her voice became distorted, as Bradley stared into her loving eyes. His mind wandered and he thought back to what Henley had said, as he recalled what would happen on his *thirteenth* birthday.

The inquisitive boy ran his fingers over the bandages covering his head, as Flaglan winked at him. The sorceress leant forward and pretended to pick up a piece of gauze from the floor, as she whispered in Bradley's ear. "Felt any lumps under those bandages yet?"

Bradley pressed harder and muttered under his breath. "Well I guess that confirms it hasn't been a bad dream... there's definitely something growing out of my head!"

Flagan winked again and produced a shiny object from her white coat pocket, as she discretely offered him another gift. "I had better give you this back now... while I've got the chance."

Bradley felt the familiar shape of the cold metal against his palm and instantly recognized the sacred grobite. He acknowledged receipt of the coin by nodding, as the boy's hearing tuned back into the sound of Margaret's excited voice. He did not have the heart to reveal the knowledge of his true identity and held out his hand to feel the warmth of his mother's slender fingers. "Good to see you again,

Mum... I hope Dad is okay too!" declared the devoted boy, as the door to the private ward creaked open and he stared nervously at the hooded stranger in the doorway.

Margaret followed her son's line of vision and turned round, as the surprise visitor removed his cloaked hood. "Henley... lovely to see you – so glad you managed to get here to see your nephew!"

"Wouldn't have missed it for the world!" replied Henley, as he placed his coat on the back of a chair.

Bradley called over to his real father in a sarcastic manner. "Which *world* would that be... *Uncle*?"

Henley asked Flaglan to move aside, as he sat on the edge of the bed and leant down to speak in a quiet tone. "Discovered your Devonian horns yet... *Son*?"

"Yes Father... just as you predicted," whispered Bradley in an excited tone.

"Well I have more news for you... it concerns a secret entrance to *Aakoria* – the fountain in Central Park has been destroyed but there could be another way into the world that holds the answer to both our prayers," uttered Henley, as he noticed the sacred grobite in Bradley's open palm.

Bradley's eyes sparkled and he clenched his fist to covet the coin, as Flaglan made sure that everyone else in the room conversed about the boy's belated birthday celebrations. The boy then confirmed his father's thoughts, as he whispered. "Are we going to find out whether *Queen Talitha* is still alive?"

Henley replied. "Anything is possible while ever you are in possession of that coin… so I guess there is a chance that the sacred grobite could provide the answer to whether your real Mother still lives!"

"How do we find the world of Aakoria?" asked Bradley, as Frannie approached her older brother.

Margaret warned her daughter not make a nuisance of herself and then asked. "Did you just mention *Australia* again, Bradley?"

"Why would I be talking to Uncle Henley about Australia?" replied Bradley and grinned.

Frannie giggled. "You were speaking about the *Queen of Australia* in your sleep!"

Bradley smiled, as he realized the significant misinterpretation of his unconscious slurring and asked his little sister to go and pester Jefferson.

Henley paused and waited for the young girl to move away again, as he delivered his answer. "The coin will reveal the whereabouts of the *Queen of Aakoria*... when the time is right!"

Bradley then asked the question that had been troubling him since he woke. "I still don't get how I ended up back in this New York time dimension!"

"The coin has great powers, Bradley... look after it – in your hands anything is possible!" replied Henley.

The conversation continued to flow inside the private ward, as a sinister looking figure peered through a round window in the door. Ethan Darke pressed his deformed face against the glass and cackled a threatening promise, as he focussed his extra-sensory powers on Bradley. "Enjoy your happy reunion, while it lasts *Baker*... for your journey to Aakoria will not be as straight forward as you think – not if I have anything to do with it!"

BRADLEY BAKER

will return in

"The Sentinel of Aarkoria"

Birds that appear as characters in this book

Jay

Robin

Kingfisher

Pigeon

Sparrow Hawk

Sand Martin

Kestrel

Bald Eagle

Green Woodpecker

Magpie

Hooded Crow

Oystercatcher

Common Gull

Great Black Backed Gull

Starling

Cormorant

Osprey

Buzzard

Tawny Owl

Parrot Crossbill

ACKNOWLEDGEMENTS

As part of the planning for this book, David Lawrence Jones worked with a group of Gifted and Talented students from schools across the Totnes Learning Community in Devon.

Creative writing workshops were hosted by the author at King Edward VI Community College.

Students were asked to create their very own character profiles from scratch and include them in a series of short adventure stories. The characters and stories were then entered into a literacy competition.

The author would like to recognize the three joint winners of the competition, whose characters appear in this book.

Keeysha Bryson, Lucy Kies and Louis Smylie Wild

BRADLEY BAKER

and the Curse of Pathylon

The first book in the series is set during the school holidays when Bradley Baker discovers a gold coin with magic powers.

"This is no ordinary coin" thought Bradley, as he is sent spinning through time to the arcane world of Pathylon... a curse has been cast and the King imprisoned inside the Shallock Tower.

Can Bradley influence the King's release, help lift the curse and escape from Pathylon alive?

ISBN: 978-0-9561499-3-0

BRADLEY BAKER

and the Amulet of Silvermoor

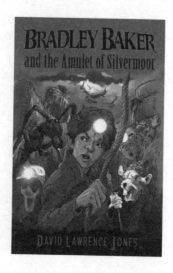

In the second book, Bradley is reunited with Sereny and Musgrove when they travel to Yorkshire during the half term break.

This time the sacred coin sends the three adventurers back to Pathylon via a derelict coal mine beneath Bradley's house. The Amulet of Silvermoor has been stolen and an ice-cloud threatens the kingdom.

Can Bradley prevent the destruction of Pathylon and stop the cloud from melting the icecaps of Freytor?

ISBN: 978-0-9561499-4-7

BRADLEY BAKER

and the Pyramids of Blood

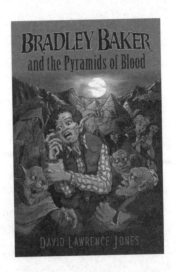

In the third book we meet a Witch, who is collaborating with the Shadow Druid to prevent Bradley dispelling the dark force that's destroying his identity.

"Without the antidote I will be transformed into an evil creature" thought Bradley, as he is sent spinning through time again in search of a sacred chalice.

Musgrove and Sereny follow their troubled friend back down the plughole, where a fallen hero has returned to help them fight the new strain of evil…

ISBN: 978-0-9561499-5-4